Stories of
CATS
WE LOVE

Stories of

CATS
WE LOVE

Seventeen tales of unforgettable feline companions

SWEETWATER
PRESS

SWEETWATER
PRESS

Stories of Cats We Love

Copyright © 2007 by Cliff Road Books, Inc.

Produced by arrangement with Sweetwater Press

ISBN-13: 978-1-58173-674-8
ISBN-10: 1-58173-674-6

Cover design by Pat Covert
Book design by Holly Smith

Table of Contents

The Cat That Walked by Himself
Rudyard Kipling

Hear and attend and listen; for this befell and behappened and became and was, O my Best Beloved, when the Tame animals were wild. The Dog was wild, and the Horse was wild, and the Cow was wild, and the Sheep was wild, and the Pig was wild—as wild as wild could be—and they walked in the Wet Wild Woods by their wild lones. But the wildest of all the wild animals was the Cat. He walked by himself, and all places were alike to him.

Of course the Man was wild too. He was dreadfully wild. He didn't even begin to be tame till he met the Woman, and she told him that she did not like living in his wild ways. She picked out a nice dry Cave, instead of a heap of wet leaves, to lie down in; and she strewed clean sand on the floor; and she lit a nice fire of wood at the back of the Cave; and she hung a dried wild-horse skin, tail-down, across the opening of the Cave; and she said, "Wipe your feet, dear, when you come in, and now we'll keep house."

That night, Best Beloved, they ate wild sheep roasted on the hot stones, and flavoured with wild garlic and wild pepper; and wild duck stuffed with wild rice and wild fenugreek and wild coriander; and marrow-bones of wild oxen; and wild cherries, and wild grenadillas. Then the Man went to sleep in front of the fire ever so happy; but the Woman sat up, combing her hair. She took the bone of the shoulder of mutton—the big fat blade-bone—and she looked at the wonderful marks on it, and she threw more wood on the fire, and she made a Magic. She made the First Singing Magic in the world.

Out in the Wet Wild Woods all the wild animals gathered together where they could see the light of the fire a long way off, and they wondered what it meant.

Then Wild Horse stamped with his wild foot and said, "O my Friends and O my Enemies, why have the Man and the Woman made that great light in that great Cave, and what harm will it do us?"

Wild Dog lifted up his wild nose and smelled the smell of roast mutton, and said, "I will go up and see and look, and say; for I think it is good. Cat, come with me."

"Nenni!" said the Cat. "I am the Cat who walks by himself, and all places are alike to me. I will not come."

"Then we can never be friends again," said Wild Dog, and he trotted off to the Cave. But when he had gone a little way the Cat said to himself, "All places are alike to me. Why should I not go too and see and look and come away at my own liking?" So he slipped after Wild Dog softly, very softly, and hid himself where he could hear everything.

When Wild Dog reached the mouth of the Cave he lifted up the dried horse-skin with his nose and sniffed the beautiful smell of the roast mutton, and the Woman, looking at the blade-bone, heard him, and laughed, and said, "Here comes the first. Wild Thing out of the Wild Woods, what do you want?"

Wild Dog said, "O my Enemy and Wife of my Enemy, what is this that smells so good in the Wild Woods?"

Then the Woman picked up a roasted mutton-bone and threw it to Wild Dog, and said, "Wild Thing out of the Wild Woods, taste and try." Wild Dog gnawed the bone, and it was more delicious than anything he had ever tasted, and he said, "O my Enemy and Wife of my Enemy, give me another."

The Woman said,"Wild Thing out of the Wild Woods, help my Man to hunt through the day and guard this Cave at night, and I will give you as many roast bones as you need."

"Ah!" said the Cat, listening. "This is a very wise Woman, but she is not so wise as I am."

Wild Dog crawled into the Cave and laid his head on the Woman's lap, and said, "O my Friend and Wife of my Friend, I will help Your Man to hunt through the day, and at night I will guard your Cave."

"Ah!" said the Cat, listening. "That is a very foolish Dog." And he went back through the Wet Wild Woods waving his wild tail, and walking by his wild lone. But he never told anybody.

When the Man waked up he said, "What is Wild Dog doing here?" And the Woman said, "His name is not Wild Dog any more, but the First Friend, because he will be our friend for always and always and always. Take him with you when you go hunting."

Next night the Woman cut great green armfuls of fresh grass from the water-meadows, and dried it before the fire, so that it smelt like new-mown hay, and she sat at the mouth of the Cave and plaited a halter out of horse-hide, and she looked at the shoulder of mutton-bone—at the big broad blade-bone—and she made a Magic. She made the Second Singing Magic in the world.

Out in the Wild Woods all the wild animals wondered what had happened to Wild Dog, and at last Wild Horse stamped with his foot and said,"I will go and see and say why Wild Dog has not returned. Cat, come with me."

"Nenni!" said the Cat. "I am the Cat who walks by himself, and all places are alike to me. I will not come." But all the same he followed Wild Horse softly, very softly, and hid himself where he could hear everything.

When the Woman heard Wild Horse tripping and stumbling on his long mane, she laughed and said, "Here comes the second. Wild Thing out of the Wild Woods what do you want?"

Wild Horse said,"O my Enemy and Wife of my Enemy, where is Wild Dog?"

The Woman laughed, and picked up the blade-bone and looked at it, and said, "Wild Thing out of the Wild Woods, you did not come here for Wild Dog, but for the sake of this good grass."

And Wild Horse, tripping and stumbling on his long mane, said, "That is true; give it to me to eat."

The Woman said, "Wild Thing out of the Wild Woods, bend your wild head and wear what I give you, and you shall eat the wonderful grass three times a day."

"Ah," said the Cat, listening, "this is a clever Woman, but she is not so clever as I am." Wild Horse bent his wild head, and the Woman slipped the plaited hide halter over it, and Wild Horse breathed on the Woman's feet and said, "O my Mistress, and Wife of my Master, I will be your servant for the sake of the wonderful grass."

"Ah," said the Cat, listening,"that is a very foolish Horse." And he went back through the Wet Wild Woods, waving his wild tail and walking by his wild lone. But he never told anybody.

When the Man and the Dog came back from hunting, the Man said, "What is Wild Horse doing here?" And the Woman said, "His name is not Wild Horse any more, but the First Servant, because he will carry us from place to place for always and always and always. Ride on his back when you go hunting."

Next day, holding her wild head high so that her wild horns should not catch in the wild trees, Wild Cow came up to the Cave, and the Cat followed, and hid himself just the same as before; and everything happened just the same as before; and the Cat said the same things as before, and when Wild Cow had promised to give her milk to the Woman every day in exchange for the wonderful grass, the Cat went back through the Wet Wild Woods waving his wild tail and walking by his wild lone, just the same as before. But he never told anybody. And when the Man and the Horse and the Dog came home from hunting and asked the same questions same as before, the Woman said, "Her name is not Wild Cow any more, but the Giver of Good Food. She will give us the warm white milk for always and always and always, and I will take care of her while you and the First Friend and the First Servant go hunting."

Next day the Cat waited to see if any other Wild thing would go up to the Cave, but no one moved in the Wet Wild Woods, so the Cat walked there by himself; and he saw the Woman milking the Cow, and he saw the light of the fire in the Cave, and he smelt the smell of the warm white milk.

Cat said, "O my Enemy and Wife of my Enemy, where did Wild Cow go?"

The Woman laughed and said, "Wild Thing out of the Wild Woods, go back to the Woods again, for I have braided up my hair, and I have put away the magic blade-bone, and we have no more need of either friends or servants in our Cave."

Cat said, "I am not a friend, and I am not a servant. I am the Cat who walks by himself, and I wish to come into your cave."

Woman said, "Then why did you not come with First Friend on the first night?"

Cat grew very angry and said, "Has Wild Dog told tales of me?"

Then the Woman laughed and said, "You are the Cat who walks by himself, and all places are alike to you. You are neither a friend nor a servant. You have said it yourself. Go away and walk by yourself in all places alike."

Then Cat pretended to be sorry and said, "Must I never come into the Cave? Must I never sit by the warm fire? Must I never drink the warm white milk? You are very wise and very beautiful. You should not be cruel even to a Cat."

Woman said, "I knew I was wise, but I did not know I was beautiful. So I will make a bargain with you. If ever I say one word in your praise you may come into the Cave."

"And if you say two words in my praise?" said the Cat.

"I never shall," said the Woman, "but if I say two words in your praise, you may sit by the fire in the Cave."

"And if you say three words?" said the Cat.

"I never shall," said the Woman, "but if I say three words in your praise, you may drink the warm white milk three times a day for always and always and always."

Then the Cat arched his back and said, "Now let the Curtain at the mouth of the Cave, and the Fire at the back of the Cave, and the Milk-pots that stand beside the Fire, remember what my Enemy and the Wife of my Enemy has said." And he went away through the Wet Wild Woods waving his wild tail and walking by his wild lone.

That night when the Man and the Horse and the Dog came home from hunting, the Woman did not tell them of the bargain that she had made with the Cat, because she was afraid that they might not like it.

Cat went far and far away and hid himself in the Wet Wild Woods by his wild lone for a long time till the Woman forgot all about him. Only the Bat—the little upside-down Bat—that hung inside the Cave, knew where Cat hid; and every evening Bat would fly to Cat with news of what was happening.

One evening Bat said, "There is a Baby in the Cave. He is new and pink and fat and small, and the Woman is very fond of him."

"Ah," said the Cat, listening, "but what is the Baby fond of?"

"He is fond of things that are soft and tickle," said the Bat. "He is fond of warm things to hold in his arms when he goes to sleep. He is fond of being played with. He is fond of all those things."

"Ah," said the Cat, listening, "then my time has come."

Next night Cat walked through the Wet Wild Woods and hid very near the Cave till morning-time, and Man and Dog and Horse went hunting. The Woman was busy cooking that morning, and the Baby cried and interrupted. So she carried him outside the Cave and gave him a handful of pebbles to play with. But still the Baby cried.

Then the Cat put out his paddy paw and patted the Baby on the cheek, and it cooed; and the Cat rubbed against its fat knees and tickled it under its fat chin with his tail. And the Baby laughed; and the Woman heard him and smiled.

Then the Bat—the little upside-down bat—that hung in the mouth of the Cave said, "O my Hostess and Wife of my Host and Mother of my Host's Son, a Wild Thing from the Wild Woods is most beautifully playing with your Baby."

"A blessing on that Wild Thing whoever he may be," said the Woman, straightening her back, "for I was a busy woman this morning and he has done me a service."

That very minute and second, Best Beloved, the dried horse-skin Curtain that was stretched tail-down at the mouth of the Cave fell down—whoosh!—because it remembered the bargain she had made with the Cat, and when the Woman went to pick it up—lo and behold!—the Cat was sitting quite comfy inside the Cave.

"O my Enemy and Wife of my Enemy and Mother of my Enemy," said the Cat, "it is I: for you have spoken a word in my praise, and now I can sit within the Cave for always and always and always. But still I am the Cat who walks by himself, and all places are alike to me."

The Woman was very angry, and shut her lips tight and took up her spinning-wheel and began to spin. But the Baby cried because the Cat had gone away, and the Woman could not hush it, for it struggled and kicked and grew black in the face.

"O my Enemy and Wife of my Enemy and Mother of my Enemy," said the Cat, "take a strand of the wire that you are spinning and tie it to your spinning-whorl and drag it along the floor, and I will show you a magic that shall make your Baby laugh as loudly as he is now crying."

"I will do so," said the Woman, "because I am at my wits' end; but I will not thank you for it."

She tied the thread to the little clay spindle whorl and drew it across the floor, and the Cat ran after it and patted it with his paws and rolled head over heels, and tossed it backward over his shoulder and chased it between his hind-legs and pretended to lose it, and pounced down upon it again, till the Baby laughed as loudly as it had been crying, and scrambled after the Cat and frolicked all over the Cave till it grew tired and settled down to sleep with the Cat in its arms.

"Now," said the Cat, "I will sing the Baby a song that shall keep him asleep for an hour." And he began to purr, loud and low, low and loud, till the Baby fell fast asleep. The Woman smiled as she looked down upon the two of them and said, "That was wonderfully done. No question but you are very clever, O Cat."

That very minute and second, Best Beloved, the smoke of the fire at the back of the Cave came down in clouds from the roof—puff!—because it remembered the bargain she had made with the Cat, and when it had cleared away—lo and behold!—the Cat was sitting quite comfy close to the fire.

"O my Enemy and Wife of my Enemy and Mother of My Enemy," said the Cat, "it is I, for you have spoken a second word in my praise, and now I can sit by the warm fire at the back of the Cave for always and always and always. But still I am the Cat who walks by himself, and all places are alike to me."

Then the Woman was very very angry, and let down her hair and put more wood on the fire and brought out the broad blade-bone of the shoulder of mutton and began to make a Magic that should prevent her from saying a third word in praise of the Cat. It was not a Singing Magic, Best Beloved, it was a Still Magic; and by and by the Cave grew so still that a little wee-wee mouse crept out of a corner and ran across the floor.

"O my Enemy and Wife of my Enemy and Mother of my Enemy," said the Cat, "is that little mouse part of your magic?"

"Ouh! Chee! No indeed!" said the Woman, and she dropped the blade-bone and jumped upon the footstool in front of the fire and braided up her hair very quick for fear that the mouse should run up it.

"Ah," said the Cat, watching, "then the mouse will do me no harm if I eat it?"

"No," said the Woman, braiding up her hair, "eat it quickly and I will ever be grateful to you."

Cat made one jump and caught the little mouse, and the Woman said, "A hundred thanks. Even the First Friend is not quick enough to catch little mice as you have done. You must be very wise."

That very moment and second, O Best Beloved, the Milk-pot that stood by the fire cracked in two pieces—ffft—because it remembered the bargain she had made with the Cat, and when the Woman jumped down from the footstool—lo and behold!—the Cat was lapping up the warm white milk that lay in one of the broken pieces.

"O my Enemy and Wife of my Enemy and Mother of my

Enemy," said the Cat, "it is I; for you have spoken three words in my praise, and now I can drink the warm white milk three times a day for always and always and always. But still I am the Cat who walks by himself, and all places are alike to me."

Then the Woman laughed and set the Cat a bowl of the warm white milk and said, "O Cat, you are as clever as a man, but remember that your bargain was not made with the Man or the Dog, and I do not know what they will do when they come home."

"What is that to me?" said the Cat. "If I have my place in the Cave by the fire and my warm white milk three times a day I do not care what the Man or the Dog can do."

That evening when the Man and the Dog came into the Cave, the Woman told them all the story of the bargain while the Cat sat by the fire and smiled. Then the Man said, "Yes, but he has not made a bargain with me or with all proper Men after me." Then he took off his two leather boots and he took up his little stone axe (that makes three) and he fetched a piece of wood and a hatchet (that is five altogether), and he set them out in a row and he said, "Now we will make our bargain. If you do not catch mice when you are in the Cave for always and always and always, I will throw these five things at you whenever I see you, and so shall all proper Men do after me."

"Ah," said the Woman, listening, "this is a very clever Cat, but he is not so clever as my Man."

The Cat counted the five things (and they looked very knobby) and he said, "I will catch mice when I am in the Cave for always and always and always; but still I am the Cat who walks by himself, and all places are alike to me."

"Not when I am near," said the Man. "If you had not said that last I would have put all these things away for always and always and always; but I am now going to throw my two boots and my little stone axe (that makes three) at you whenever I meet you. And so shall all proper Men do after me!"

Then the Dog said, "Wait a minute. He has not made a bargain with me or with all proper Dogs after me." And he showed his teeth and said, "If you are not kind to the Baby while I am in the Cave for always and always and always, I will hunt you till I catch you, and when I catch you I will bite you. And so shall all proper Dogs do after me."

"Ah," said the Woman, listening, "this is a very clever Cat, but he is not so clever as the Dog."

Cat counted the Dog's teeth (and they looked very pointed) and he said, "I will be kind to the Baby while I am in the Cave, as long as he does not pull my tail too hard, for always and always and always. But still I am the Cat that walks by himself, and all places are alike to me."

"Not when I am near," said the Dog. "If you had not said that last I would have shut my mouth for always and always and always; but now I am going to hunt you up a tree whenever I meet you. And so shall all proper Dogs do after me."

Then the Man threw his two boots and his little stone axe (that makes three) at the Cat, and the Cat ran out of the Cave and the Dog chased him up a tree; and from that day to this, Best Beloved, three proper Men out of five will always throw things at a Cat whenever they meet him, and all proper Dogs will chase him up a tree. But the Cat keeps his side of the bargain too. He will kill mice and he will be kind to Babies when he is in the house, just as long as they do not pull his tail too hard. But when he has done that, and between times, and when the moon gets up and night comes, he is the Cat that walks by himself, and all places are alike to him. Then he goes out to the Wet Wild Woods or up the Wet Wild Trees or on the Wet Wild Roofs, waving his wild tail and walking by his wild lone.

Pussy can sit by the fire and sing,
　Pussy can climb a tree,
Or play with a silly old cork and string
　To'muse herself, not me.
But I like Binkie my dog, because
　He knows how to behave;
So, Binkie's the same as the First Friend was,
　And I am the Man in the Cave.

Pussy will play man-Friday till
　It's time to wet her paw
And make her walk on the window-sill
　(For the footprint Crusoe saw);
Then she fluffles her tail and mews,
　And scratches and won't attend.
But Binkie will play whatever I choose,
　And he is my true First Friend.

Pussy will rub my knees with her head
　Pretending she loves me hard;
But the very minute I go to my bed
　Pussy runs out in the yard,
And there she stays till the morning-light;
　So I know it is only pretend;
But Binkie, he snores at my feet all night,
　And he is my Firstest Friend!

The White Cat

There once was a ageing king who had three brave and clever sons. The king did not wish to give up his throne just yet, and was afraid that his sons would want to reign over the kingdom before he was dead. He decided to divert the minds of his sons by promises which he could always get out of when the time came for keeping them. So he sent for them all, and, after speaking to them kindly, he added: "I'm sure you'll agree that my great age makes it impossible for me to look after my affairs of state as carefully as I once did. Hence I wish that one of you should succeed me, but in return you should do something for me. I'm thinking of retiring into the country and it seems that a faithful little dog would be good company for me. Whichever of you brings me the prettiest little dog shall succeed me at once."

The three princes were surprised by their father's sudden fancy for a little dog, but as the challenge gave the two younger princes an unexpected chance of being king, and as the eldest was too polite to object, they eagerly accepted the challenge. They bade farewell to the king, who gave them presents of silver and gems, and he arranged to meet them in one year's time, at the same time and place, to see the little dogs they had brought for him.

The princes and their retainers went together to a castle one league from the city, where they enjoyed a grand banquet. The three brothers promised to remain firm friends, to share whatever good fortune befell them, and not to be parted by envy or jealousy. Each one took a different road, and though the two eldest met with many adventures, this tale concerns the adventures of the youngest prince.

The young prince was handsome and merry, brave and versed in everything a prince should know. He wandered from place to place and hardly a day passed without his buying several dogs of all sizes and breeds. Each time he bought a pretty one he would spy one prettier still and then have to sell all the others for it was quite impossible for him to take a thousand dogs with him on his travels!

One nightfall, he reached a great, gloomy forest. He was quickly lost and, to make matters worse, a storm began. He took the first path he saw and, after walking for a long time, he saw a faint red light and hoped to find some woodcutter's cottage where he could shelter for the night. At length, guided by the light, he reached the golden door of the most splendid castle imaginable. Its walls were fine porcelain in most delicate colours, and the prince saw that all the stories he had ever read were pictured upon them. He was too wet and miserable to spend long looking about and he went to the great golden door.

There he saw a deer's foot hanging by a diamond chain and he wondered who could live in this magnificent castle and not worry about the diamond chain being stolen. He pulled the deer's foot, and immediately a silver bell sounded and the door flew open. The Prince could see nothing but numbers of soft, pretty hands in the air, each holding a flaming torch. He was so surprised that he stood quite still until the hands pushed him into a hall paved with lapis-lazuli, while two lovely voices sang: "The hands you see floating above will swiftly your bidding obey; If your heart dreads not conquering Love, in this place you may fearlessly stay."

The White Cat

No longer afraid, the prince allowed the hands to guide him towards a door of coral, which opened of its own accord, and he found himself in a vast hall of mother-of-pearl, out of which opened a many other brightly lit and fabulously equipped rooms. After passing through some sixty rooms, he reached a comfortable-looking armchair drawn up close to a hearth which sprang alight as he approached. The hands, which often appeared quite suddenly and unexpectedly, took off his wet, muddy clothes and dressed him in rich clothes embroidered with gold and emeralds.

The hands then led him to a splendid room, decorated with tapestries and paintings of Puss in Boots and other famous cats. The table was laid for supper with two golden plates, and golden spoons and forks, and the sideboard was covered with bejewelled dishes and glasses of crystal. The prince wondered who the second place could be for. Suddenly in came about a dozen cats carrying guitars and music; they took their places at one end of the room, and under the direction of a cat who beat time with a roll of paper, the cat musicians began to mew in every imaginable key and to draw their claws across the strings of the guitars, making the strangest kind of music the prince had ever heard. At first he put his fingers in his ears, but soon he was overcome with laughter at the comical sight and he wondered what funny sight he would see next.

Instantly the door opened, and in came a tiny figure covered by a long black veil. It was conducted by two cats wearing black mantles and carrying swords, and a large party of cats followed, who brought in cages full of rats and mice. At first, the astonished prince thought he was dreaming, but the little figure came up to him and threw back its veil to reveal the loveliest little white cat imaginable. She looked very young and very sad, and in a sweet little voice that went straight to his heart she spoke to him.

"King's son," said the sad white cat, "You are welcome. The Queen of the Cats is glad to see you."

"Lady Cat," replied the prince, "I thank you for receiving me so kindly, but surely you are no ordinary cat? The way you speak and the magnificence of your castle prove it plainly."

"King's son," said the white cat, "I am not used to such compliments. Let supper be served and let my musicians be silent, as the prince does not understand what they are saying."

The mysterious hands brought in the supper. First they put on the table two dishes, one containing stewed pigeons and the other a fricassee of fat mice. The sight of mice made the prince feel uneasy, but the white cat assured him that his own dishes had been prepared in a separate kitchen and he could be certain they contained no rats or mice. Sure she would not deceive him, the prince began to eat.

Presently he noticed that the white cat wore on her little paw a bracelet containing a portrait. He begged to be allowed to look at it. To his great surprise he found the portrait depicted a handsome young man who bore an uncanny resemblance to himself. The white cat sighed and seemed sadder than ever, so the prince dared not ask about the portrait. Instead, he talked of other things and found that she was interested in the same subjects that interested him.

After supper they went into another room, which was equipped as a theatre, and the cats acted and danced for their amusement. At length, the white cat bade him good-night and the hands conducted him into a room hung with tapestry worked with butterflies' wings of every colour and with mirrors from floor to ceiling and a little white bed with curtains of gauze tied up with ribbons.

In the morning he was awakened by a noise and confusion outside of his window, and the mysterious hands quickly dressed him in hunting costume. When he looked out, all the cats were assembled in the courtyard, some leading greyhounds, some blowing horns, for the white cat was going out hunting. The hands led a wooden horse up to the prince, and mounted him on it despite his protests. It at once pranced gaily off with him.

The white cat rode a monkey, which climbed even up to the eagles' nests when she desired young eaglets. Never was there a pleasanter hunting party, and when they returned to the castle the prince and the white cat dined together as before. This time, after the meal was done, she offered him a crystal goblet, which must have contained a magic draught, for, as soon as he had swallowed its contents, he forgot everything, even the little dog that he was seeking for the king. His only thought was how happy he was to be with the white cat.

The days passed in every kind of amusement, until the year was nearly gone. The prince had forgotten about the meeting with his brothers and had even forgotten what country he belonged to. The white cat knew when he ought to go back, and one day she said to him: "Do you know that you have only three days left to look for the little dog for your father, and your brothers have found lovely ones?"

The prince's memory returned at once and he cried, "What can have made me forget such an important thing? My whole fortune depends upon it! There is no time to find a dog pretty enough to gain me a kingdom and I am far more than three days away from my home!"

The prince was distraught, but the white cat said to him: "King's son, do not fret. I am your friend and will make everything easy for you. Stay another day as the wooden horse can take you to your father in twelve hours."

"Thank you, beautiful Cat," replied the prince, "but there is little point as I have no dog to take to my father."

"See here," answered the white cat, holding up an acorn, "This acorn holds a prettier one than in the Dogstar!"

The prince chastised the white cat for teasing him, but she held the acorn to his ear and he heard a tiny "woof woof" from inside it. The prince was delighted, for it must surely be the smallest dog ever. He wanted to take it out to see it, but the white cat told him to wait until he was before the king, and in any case the tiny dog might become cold on the journey. So he stayed with her another day and thanked her a thousand times.

At last, time came for him to return home and he sadly said goodbye and said to the white cat, "The days here have passed so quickly! I wish I could take you with me." But the white cat just sighed sadly and shook her head.

He was the first of the three princes to arrive at the castle. His brothers looked questioningly at the prancing wooden horse, but he kept quiet about his own adventures while listening to their stories. When they asked what dog he'd brought, he showed them a misshapen turnspit dog. The two elder princes smiled secretly, knowing their dogs to be far prettier than the ugly turnspit dog.

The brothers set out together in a coach. The elder brothers carried dogs so tiny and fragile they hardly dared touch them. The turnspit dog ran behind the coach and was filthy with mud by the time they arrived at the palace. The king could not decide which of the two tiny dogs was the prettier and while the elder brothers were arranging how to divide the kingdom up between them, their youngest brother stepped forward and opened the acorn. Inside, on a white cushion, was a dog so small that it could easily have jumped through a finger ring. The king complained that he could not decide which dog was prettiest and would therefore have to set another task in order to reach a decision.

He asked them to find him a piece of muslin so fine that it could be drawn through the eye of a needle. The brothers consented, though less willingly than before, and set out. The youngest mounted on his wooden horse and rode at full speed back to his beloved white cat. Back at the fabulous castle staffed by the mysterious hands, he found her asleep in a little basket on a white satin cushion. She was overjoyed at seeing him once more.

"How could I hope that you would come back to me King's son?" she said.

As he stroked and petted her, he told her that the king could not reach a decision and had set a new task. The white cat looked serious and said she must think what was to be done, though luckily she knew cats in the castle who could spin very well. Then they danced and dined together, and watched magnificent fireworks from a gallery overlooking the river.

The days passed quickly as before and it was impossible to be bored as the white cat had a talent for inventing new amusements. When the prince asked her how it was that she was so wise, she only said, "King's son, do not ask me, but guess what you please. I may not tell you anything."

The prince was so happy that he lost track of time until the white cat told him that the year was gone and it was time for him to return to his own palace. Her spinning cats had made the piece of muslin very well.

"This time," she said, "I can give you a suitable escort," and in the courtyard the prince found a golden chariot enamelled with red and drawn by twelve snow-white horses, harnessed four abreast. A hundred chariots followed, each drawn by eight horses, and filled with officers in splendid uniforms, while a thousand guards surrounded the procession.

"Go!" said the White Cat, "and when you appear before the

King in such state he surely will not refuse you the crown which you deserve. Take this walnut, but do not open it until you are before him, then you will find in it the piece of stuff you asked me for."

"Lovely Blanchette," said the prince, for that was what he had named the white cat, "however can I thank you for your kindness? Just say the words and I will give up all thought of kingship and stay here with you forever."

"King's son," she replied, "you are kind to care so much for a little white mouse-catcher, but you must not stay."

The prince kissed her little white paw and set out. The enchanted chariots reached the king's palace in just six hours. This time his brothers had arrived first and had impressed the king with their pieces of muslin which they felt sure would pass through the eye of a needle. However, the wily king sent for a particular needle with such a tiny eye that everyone could see the muslin would never pass through it.

The two princes were angry and began to complain that it was an unfair trick. Just then, the youngest prince came in and his father and brothers were quite astonished at his magnificence. He took out the walnut and opened it, expecting to find a piece of muslin. Inside the walnut he found a hazelnut and inside that was a cherry stone and inside that was a grain of wheat. The prince thought the white cat had played a joke, but he quite distinctly felt a cat's claw scratch his hand so he opened the grain of wheat and found a millet seed. Inside the millet seed he drew out a piece of muslin four hundred ells long, woven with gorgeous colours and patterns. This muslin went through the needle's eye six times with ease. The king turned pale and other princes were silent. No-one could deny that this was the finest piece of muslin that was to be found in the world.

Presently the king turned to his sons, and said, with a deep sigh, "If you are to rule my kingdom, you need a queen to rule beside you. Go forth once more and whoever at the end of a year can bring back the loveliest princess shall be king and queen."

Though he had clearly won the challenge, the prince went back to his chariot and he and his escort returned to the white cat faster than he had left. This time she was expecting him. The path was strewn with flowers and a braziers of scented woods perfumed the air.

"Well, King's son," she said, "here you are again without a crown."

"Madam Blanchette," he sighed, "thanks to your generosity I have earned my crown twice over, but my wily father is so loath to part with it that it would give me no pleasure to have it."

Blanchette replied, "As you must next take back a lovely princess with you I will be on the look-out for one for you. Meanwhile let us enjoy ourselves."

The year slipped away even more pleasantly than the previous ones. Sometimes the prince could not help asking Blanchette how it was she could talk, "Perhaps you are a fairy, or some enchanter changed you into a cat?"

The white cat only gave him answers that told him nothing and while they were together he was so happy he quite lost track of time. One evening, the white cat told him that if he wanted to take a lovely princess home with him the next day he must be prepared to do exactly what she told him. Although he loved no-one, but Blanchette, he knew he could not wed a cat and he agreed.

"Take your sword," she said, "and cut off my head!"

"I cannot!" cried the prince, "How can you even ask such a thing?"

"Please do it," Blanchette begged.

Though he begged her to ask him to set a different task to prove his devotion to her, nothing could change her mind. He took out his sword and with tears running down his cheeks and a trembling hand, he cut off her little white head. Suddenly a lovely princess stood before him. While he was speechless with amazement, the door opened and a goodly company of knights and ladies entered, each carrying a cat's skin. They each kissed the princess's hand and congratulated her on being restored to her own form. After a short while she asked to be alone with the prince.

"You were right in supposing me to be no ordinary cat. My father reigned over six kingdoms. The queen, my mother, whom he loved dearly, had a passion for travelling and exploring, and when I was only a few weeks old she obtained his permission to visit a certain mountain of which she had heard many marvellous tales. She set out, taking with her a number of her attendants. On the way they passed near an old castle belonging to the fairies. Nobody had ever been into it, but it was reported to be full of the most wonderful things and its garden was reputed to have such fruits as were to be found nowhere else. She wished to try these fruits for herself. Though her servants knocked and rang at the door, no-one answered and they believed the castle's inhabitants either asleep or dead. By then she was determined to try the fruit so she ordered her servants to put ladders against the wall and climb over. Though the walls did not look very high, however many ladders they tied together, they could not reach the top.

The queen was sick with disappointment. She ordered her servants to set up camp for the night so they could try something else in the morning. In the middle of the night she was suddenly awakened by a tiny, ugly old woman. The old woman said to my mother, "It is somewhat troublesome of your Majesty to insist upon tasting our fruit. To save further annoyance, my sisters and I will give you as much as you can carry away, on one condition—you shall give us your little daughter to bring up as our own."

Though the queen begged the old fairy to take some other gift in return—kingdoms to rule, or riches, the old fairy insisted that only the baby daughter would do. "She shall be as happy as the day is long, and we will give her everything that is worth having in fairy-land, but you must not see her again until she is married." The queen consented, for she thought she would die of despair if she did not taste the fruit and so would lose her baby daughter either way.

The old fairy led her into the beautiful castle and called for the fruit to be brought to her. Golden baskets of perfect apricots, peaches, nectarines, cherries, plums, pears, melons, grapes, apples, oranges, lemons, gooseberries, strawberries, and raspberries appeared at once.

The queen gave up her plan to visit the mountain and returned to her kingdom, but before she had gone very far she regretted her bargain. When the king came out to meet her she looked so sad that he guessed that something had happened, and asked what was the matter. The queen was afraid to tell him, but all at once five ugly dwarfs arrived to collect the baby princess and the queen told him about the fruit. In anger, the king drove the dwarfs away and had locked his queen and the baby princess in a securely guarded tower.

Then the fairies sent a great dragon which killed the king's subjects and devastated the kingdom until the king agreed to hand over his baby daughter to the fairies. The fairies took away the baby daughter—that is myself—and led away the dragon. I grew up in a fine tower surrounded with everything that was beautiful and rare, and learning everything that is ever taught to a princess, but without any companions but a talking parrot and a talking dog. I was visited each day by one of the old fairies and believed myself to be the fairies' own child, knowing nothing of my mother's bargain.

One day, as I sat at my window I saw a handsome young prince who had come hunting in the forest around my tower. He saluted me with great deference and I was delighted to have some one new to talk to. Despite the height of my window, we talked until nightfall. He visited me many times and I consented to marry him, but the question was how was I to escape from my tower. The fairies always supplied me with flax for spinning so I made enough cord for a ladder that reached to the foot of the tower. Just as my prince was helping me descend it, the crossest and ugliest of the old fairies caught us and the young prince was swallowed up by the fairies' dragon.

The fairies were furious at having their plans thwarted. They had intended me to marry the king of the dwarfs. When I utterly refused, they changed me into a white cat and brought me here. All the lords and ladies of my father's court were here too, some made into cats and the ones of lowest rank made invisible except for their hands. The fairies then told me all my history and warned me that my only chance of regaining my natural form was to win the love of a prince who resembled in every way my unfortunate lover."

"And you have won it, lovely Princess," interrupted the prince.

"You are indeed wonderfully like him," said Blanchette, "and if you really love me all my troubles will be at an end."

"I love you more than anything and my troubles will also be ended if you will consent to marry me," said the prince, on bended knee.

They mounted into the golden chariot together and the journey was utterly delightful as they were together. At the prince's father's palace, four guards carried the princess in a crystal sedan chair with silk curtains drawn so that no-one could see her. The two older princes had each returned with a lovely princess, but the younger prince smiled and said he had returned with a rarer prize—a white cat. They just laughed at him and asked if had taken a cat for a wife because he was afraid of mice. Then the princes went to present their brides to their father.

"Are the ladies beautiful?" asked the king anxiously.

The two older princes answered that nobody had ever before seen such lovely princesses, which made the king quite annoyed. However the king could not choose which of their princesses was the most beautiful. Finally he turned to his youngest son.

"Have you come back without a bride?"

"Your Majesty, my father" replied the prince, "in that crystal chair you will find a little white cat, which has such soft paws, and mews so prettily, that I am sure you will be charmed with it."

The king smiled and went to draw back the curtains himself, but at a touch from the princess the crystal shattered and she stood in all her beauty. Her fair hair floated over her shoulders and was crowned with flowers. Her robe was purest white.

"Sire," said Blanchette, "I will not deprive you of the throne you fill so worthily. I have already six kingdoms. Permit me to bestow one upon you and one upon each of your sons. I ask nothing but your friendship, and your consent to my marriage with your youngest son. We shall still have three kingdoms for ourselves."

The king could not conceal his joy and astonishment and the three princes were married at once to their princesses. After many months of celebration, each king and queen departed to their own kingdom and lived happily ever after, but only one of their castles was ever after full of cats.

The Woman and the Cat
Marcel Prevost

Yes," said our old friend Tribourdeaux, a man of culture and a philosopher, which is a combination rarely found among army surgeons; "yes, the supernatural is everywhere; it surrounds us and hems us in and permeates us. If science pursues it, it takes flight and cannot be grasped. Our intellect resembles those ancestors of ours who cleared a few acres of forest; whenever they approached the limits of their clearing they heard low growls and saw gleaming eyes everywhere circling them about. I myself have had the sensation of having approached the limits of the unknown several times in my life, and on one occasion in particular."

A young lady present interrupted him:

"Doctor, you are evidently dying to tell us a story. Come now, begin!"

The doctor bowed.

"No, I am not in the least anxious, I assure you. I tell this story as seldom as possible, for it disturbs those who hear it, and it disturbs me also. However, if you wish it, here it is:

"In 1863 I was a young physician stationed at Orleans. In that patrician city, full of aristocratic old residences, it is difficult to find bachelor apartments; and, as I like both plenty of air and plenty of room, I took up my lodging on the first floor of a large building situated just outside the city, near Saint-Euverte. It had been originally constructed to serve as the warehouse and also as the dwelling of a manufacturer of rugs. In course of time the manufacturer had failed, and this big barrack that he had built, falling out of repair through lack of tenants, had been sold for a song with all its furnishings. The purchaser hoped to make a future profit out of his purchase, for the city was growing in that direction; and, as a matter of fact, I believe that at the present time the house is included within the city limits. When I took up my quarters there, however, the mansion stood alone on the verge of the open country, at the end of a straggling street on which a few stray houses produced at dusk the impression of a jaw from which most of the teeth have fallen out.

"I leased one-half of the first floor, an apartment of four rooms. For my bedroom and my study I took the two that fronted on the street; in the third room I set up some shelves for my wardrobe, and the other room I left empty. This made a very comfortable lodging for me, and I had, for a sort of promenade, a broad balcony that ran along the entire front of the building, or rather one-half of the balcony, since it was divided into two parts (please note this carefully) by a fan of ironwork, over which, however, one could easily climb.

"I had been living there for about two months when, one night in July on returning to my rooms, I saw with a good deal of surprise a light shining through the windows of the other apartment on the same floor, which I had supposed to be uninhabited. The effect of this light was extraordinary. It lit up with a pale, yet perfectly distinct, reflection, parts of the balcony, the street below, and a bit of the neighboring fields.

"I thought to myself, 'Aha! I have a neighbor.'

"The idea indeed was not altogether agreeable, for I had been rather proud of my exclusive proprietorship. On reaching my bedroom I passed noiselessly out upon the balcony, but already the light had been extinguished. So I went back into my room, and sat down to read for an hour or two. From time to time I seemed to hear about me, as though within the walls, light footsteps; but after finishing my book I went to bed, and speedily fell asleep.

"About midnight I suddenly awoke with a curious feeling that something was standing beside me. I raised myself in bed, lit a candle, and this is what I saw. In the middle of the room stood an immense cat gazing upon me with phosphorescent eyes, and with its back slightly arched. It was a magnificent Angora, with long fur and a fluffy tail, and of a remarkable color—exactly like that of the yellow silk that one sees in cocoons—so that, as the light gleamed upon its coat, the animal seemed to be made of gold.

"It slowly moved toward me on its velvety paws, softly rubbing its sinuous body against my legs. I leaned over to stroke it, and it permitted my caress, purring, and finally leaping upon my knees. I noticed then that it was a female cat, quite young, and that she seemed disposed to permit me to pet her as long as ever I would. Finally, however, I put her down upon the floor, and tried to induce her to leave the room; but she leaped away from me and hid herself somewhere among the furniture, though as soon as I had blown out my candle, she jumped upon my bed. Being sleepy, however, I didn't molest her, but dropped off into a doze, and the next morning when I awoke in broad daylight I could find no sign of the animal at all.

"Truly, the human brain is a very delicate instrument, and one that is easily thrown out of gear. Before I proceed, just sum up for yourselves the facts that I have mentioned: a light seen and presently extinguished in an apartment supposed to be uninhabited; and a cat of a remarkable color, which appeared and disappeared in a way that was slightly mysterious. Now there isn't anything very strange about that, is there? Very well. Imagine, now, that these unimportant facts are repeated day after day and under the same conditions throughout a whole week, and then, believe me, they become of importance enough to impress the mind of a man who is living all alone, and to produce in him a slight disquietude such as I spoke of in commencing my story, and such as is always caused when one approaches the sphere of the unknown. The human mind is so formed that it always unconsciously applies the principle of the causa sufficiens. For every series of facts that are identical, it demands a cause, a law; and a vague dismay seizes upon it when it is unable to guess this cause and to trace out this law.

"I am no coward, but I have often studied the manifestation of fear in others, from its most puerile form in children up to its most tragic phase in madmen. I know that it is fed and nourished by uncertainties, although when one actually sets himself to investigate the cause, this fear is often transformed into simple curiosity.

"I made up my mind, therefore, to ferret out the truth. I questioned my caretaker, and found that he knew nothing about my neighbors. Every morning an old woman came to look after the neighboring apartment; my caretaker had tried to question her, but either she was completely deaf or else she was unwilling to give him any information, for she had refused to answer a single word. Nevertheless, I was able to explain satisfactorily the first thing that I had noted—that is to say, the sudden extinction of the light at the moment when I entered the house. I had observed that the windows next to mine were covered only by long lace curtains; and as the two balconies were connected, my neighbor, whether man or woman, had no doubt a wish to prevent any indiscreet inquisitiveness on my part, and therefore had always put out the light on hearing me come in. To verify this supposition, I tried a very simple experiment, which succeeded perfectly. I had a cold supper brought in one day about noon by my servant, and that evening I did not go out. When darkness came on, I took my station near the window. Presently I saw the balcony shining with the light that streamed through the windows of the neighboring apartment. At once I slipped quietly out upon my balcony, and stepped softly over the ironwork that separated the two parts. Although I knew that I was exposing myself to a positive danger, either of falling and breaking my neck, or of finding myself face to face with a man, I experienced no perturbation. Reaching the lighted window without having made the slightest noise, I found it partly open; its curtains, which for me were quite transparent since I was on the dark side of the window, made me wholly invisible to any one who should look toward the window from the interior of the room.

"I saw a vast chamber furnished quite elegantly, though it was obviously out of repair, and lighted by a lamp suspended from the ceiling. At the end of the room was a low sofa upon which was reclining a woman who seemed to me to be both young and pretty. Her loosened hair fell over her shoulders in a rain of gold. She was looking at herself in a hand mirror, patting herself, passing her arms over her lips, and twisting about her supple body with a curiously feline grace. Every movement that she made caused her long hair to ripple in glistening undulations.

"As I gazed upon her I confess that I felt a little troubled, especially when all of a sudden the young girl's eyes were fixed upon me—strange eyes, eyes of a phosphorescent green that gleamed like the flame of a lamp. I was sure that I was invisible, being on the dark side of a curtained window. That was simple enough, yet nevertheless I felt that I was seen. The girl, in fact, uttered a cry, and then turned and buried her face in the sofa-pillows.

"I raised the window, rushed into the room toward the sofa, and leaned over the face that she was hiding. As I did so, being really very remorseful, I began to excuse and to accuse myself, calling myself all sorts of names, and begging pardon for my indiscretion. I said that I deserved to be driven from her presence, but begged not to be sent away without at least a word of pardon. For a long time I pleaded thus without success, but at last she slowly turned, and I saw that her fair young face was stirred with just the faintest suggestion of a smile. When she caught a glimpse of me she murmured something of which I did not then quite get the meaning.

"'It is you,' she cried out; 'it is you!'

"As she said this, and as I looked at her, not knowing yet exactly what to answer, I was harassed by the thought: Where on earth have I already seen this face, this look, this very gesture? Little by little, however, I found my tongue, and after saying a few more words in apology for my unpardonable curiosity, and getting brief but not offended answers, I took leave of her, and, retiring through the window by which I had come, went back to my own room. Arriving there, I sat a long time by the window in the darkness, charmed by the face that I had seen, and yet singularly disquieted. This woman so beautiful, so amiable, living so near to me, who said to me, 'It is you,' exactly as though she had already known me, who spoke so little, who answered all my questions with evasion, excited in me a feeling of fear. She had, indeed, told me her name— Linda—and that was all. I tried in vain to drive away the remembrance of her greenish eyes, which in the darkness seemed still to gleam upon me, and of those glints which, like electric sparks, shone in her long hair whenever she stroked it with her hand. Finally, however, I retired for the night; but scarcely was my head upon the pillow when I felt some moving body descend upon my feet. The cat had appeared again. I tried to chase her away, but she kept returning again and again, until I ended by resigning myself to her presence; and, just as before, I went to sleep with this strange companion near me. Yet my rest was this time a troubled one, and broken by strange and fitful dreams.

"Have you ever experienced the sort of mental obsession which gradually causes the brain to be mastered by some single absurd idea—an idea almost insane, and one which your reason and your will alike repel, but which nevertheless gradually blends itself with your thought, fastens itself upon your mind, and grows and grows? I suffered cruelly in this way on the days that followed my strange adventure. Nothing new occurred, but in the evening, going out upon the balcony, I found Linda standing upon her side of the iron fan. We chatted together for a while in the half darkness, and, as before, I returned to my room to find that in a few moments the golden cat appeared, leaped upon my bed, made a nest for herself there, and remained until the morning. I knew now to whom the cat belonged, for Linda had answered that very same evening, on my speaking of it, 'Oh, yes, my cat; doesn't she look exactly as though she were made of gold?' As I said, nothing new had occurred, yet nevertheless a vague sort of terror began little by little to master me and to develop itself in my mind, at first merely as a bit of foolish fancy, and then as a haunting belief that dominated my entire thought, so that I perpetually seemed to see a thing which it was in reality quite impossible to see."

"Why, it's easy enough to guess," interrupted the young lady who had spoken at the beginning of his story. "Linda and the cat were the same thing."

Tribourdeaux smiled.

"I should not have been quite so positive as that," he said, "even then; but I cannot deny that this ridiculous fancy haunted me for many hours when I was endeavoring to snatch a little sleep amid the insomnia that a too active brain produced. Yes, there were moments when these two beings with greenish eyes, sinuous movements, golden hair, and mysterious ways, seemed to me to be blended into one, and to be merely the double manifestation of a single entity. As I said, I saw Linda again and again, but in spite of all my efforts to come upon her unexpectedly, I never was able to see them both at the same time. I tried to reason with myself, to convince myself that there was nothing really inexplicable in all of this, and I ridiculed myself for being afraid both of a woman and of a harmless cat. In truth, at the end of all my reasoning, I found that I was not so much afraid of the animal alone or of the woman alone, but rather of a sort of quality which existed in my fancy and inspired me with a fear of something that was incorporeal—fear of a manifestation of my own spirit, fear of a vague thought, which is, indeed, the very worst of fears.

"I began to be mentally disturbed. After long evenings spent in confidential and very unconventional chats with Linda, in which little by little my feelings took on the color of love, I passed long days of secret torment, such as incipient maniacs must experience. Gradually a resolve began to grow up in my mind, a desire that became more and more importunate in demanding a solution of this unceasing and tormenting doubt; and the more I cared for Linda, the more it seemed absolutely necessary to push this resolve to its fulfillment. I decided to kill the cat.

"One evening before meeting Linda on the balcony, I took out of my medical cabinet a jar of glycerin and a small bottle of hydrocyanic acid, together with one of those little pencils of glass which chemists use in mixing certain corrosive substances. That evening for the first time Linda allowed me to caress her. I held her in my arms and passed my hand over her long hair, which snapped

40

and cracked under my touch in a succession of tiny sparks. As soon as I regained my room the golden cat, as usual, appeared before me. I called her to me; she rubbed herself against me with arched back and extended tail, purring the while with the greatest amiability. I took the glass pencil in my hand, moistened the point in the glycerin, and held it out to the animal, which licked it with her long red tongue. I did this three or four times, but the next time I dipped the pencil in the acid. The cat unhesitatingly touched it with her tongue. In an instant she became rigid, and a moment after, a frightful titanic convulsion caused her to leap thrice into the air, and then to fall upon the floor with a dreadful cry—a cry that was truly human. She was dead!

"With the perspiration starting from my forehead and with trembling hands I threw myself upon the floor beside the body that was not yet cold. The starting eyes had a look that froze me with horror. The blackened tongue was thrust out between the teeth; the limbs exhibited the most remarkable contortions. I mustered all my courage with a violent effort of will, took the animal by the paws, and left the house. Hurrying down the silent street, I proceeded to the quays along the banks of the Loire, and, on reaching them, threw my burden into the river. Until daylight I roamed around the city, just where I know not; and not until the sky began to grow pale and then to be flushed with light did I at last have the courage to return home. As I laid my hand upon the door, I shivered. I had a dread of finding there still living, as in the celebrated tale of Poe, the animal that I had so lately put to death. But no, my room was empty. I fell half-fainting upon my bed, and for the first time I slept, with a perfect sense of being all alone, a sleep like that of a beast or of an assassin, until evening came."

Some one here interrupted, breaking in upon the profound silence in which we had been listening.

"I can guess the end. Linda disappeared at the same time as the cat."

"You see perfectly well," replied Tribourdeaux, "that there exists between the facts of this story a curious coincidence, since you are able to guess so exactly their relation. Yes, Linda disappeared. They found in her apartment her dresses, her linen, all even to the night-robe that she was to have worn that night, but there was nothing that could give the slightest clue to her identity. The owner of the house had let the apartment to 'Mademoiselle Linda, concert-singer.' He knew nothing more. I was summoned before the police magistrate. I had been seen on the night of her disappearance roaming about with a distracted air in the vicinity of the river. Luckily the judge knew me; luckily also, he was a man of no ordinary intelligence. I related to him privately the entire story, just as I have been telling it to you. He dismissed the inquiry; yet I may say that very few have ever had so narrow an escape as mine from a criminal trial."

For several moments the silence of the company was unbroken. Finally a gentleman, wishing to relieve the tension, cried out:

"Come now, doctor, confess that this is really all fiction; that you merely want to prevent these ladies from getting any sleep to-night."

Tribourdeaux bowed stiffly, his face unsmiling and a little pale.

"You may take it as you will," he said.

How Cats Got Their Purr

There once lived a king and queen who longed for a baby daughter. Finally, just as they were giving up hope, the queen bore a girl child and the king and queen were the happiest people on earth. Only one thing marred their contentment. A gypsy witch had read the queen's fortune in return for some food from the royal kitchen and she had predicted that the child would be a girl. The gypsy had given the queen a dire warning and in anger the king had driven the old crone from his land. The old woman's warning weighed heavily on their hearts.

The old witch had said: "You will bear a daughter and she will be strong and healthy. However, she will fall dead if she ever gives her hand in marriage to a prince. Heed my advice. Find three pure white cats, with not a single colored hair upon them, and let them grow up with your child. Give the cats balls of two types to play with—balls of gold and balls of linen thread. If they ignore the gold and play with the linen, all will be well, but should they ignore the linen and choose the gold, beware!"

The king sent out a royal decree and his subjects offered him cats and kittens of all types—tabby cats, ginger tomcats, tortoiseshell mother cats still nursing their kittens; he was offered black kittens, grey kittens and ginger kittens. All of these he sent away again, being only interested in three pure cats. After years of searching, three white cats without a single colored hair were duly found and though they came from different places, they became good friends. The three cats loved their young mistress and she adored them. As the months turned into years, the linen balls continued to be the only toys the cats chose to play with. The gold balls lay dusty and forgotten.

When the princess grew old enough to learn how to spin the cats were happy as she was. They leaped at the wheel as it turned and at the thread as the princess spun it, behaving like kittens. She begged her playful cats to leave things alone but they ignored her and continued to play gaily. The queen was so happy that the cats played only with the linen balls and never with the gold balls that she simply laughed at their antics and frolics.

At sixteen years old, the princess was very beautiful. Princes from neighbouring kingdoms and further afield asked her hand in marriage, but she remained indifferent to them all. She was content to live with her three beloved cats. One day, however, a prince arrived who was good and charming, wise and handsome, kind and virtuous and the princess fell deeply in love with him. Though he brought her gifts and visited often, he never once asked for her hand in marriage. One day she could bear it no longer and she confessed her love for him. Delighted and surprise, he expressed his own love for her.

The three white cats were in the tower room playing with the linen balls, but no sooner had the prince and princess professed their love for each other, than the cats seemed to notice the gold balls for the first time ever and began to play with them. In horror, servants reported the dire news to the king and queen. However, it wasn't the princess who was struck down but the prince. He became gravely ill and nothing the physicians did could ease or cure whatever malady had struck him down.

In desperation the princess sought the gypsy who had made the prophecy about the cats and balls. The gypsy witch told her that there was only one way to save the prince. The princess must spin ten thousand skeins of pure white linen thread before midwinter's day. It was an impossible task—only twenty-seven days remained before midwinter's day. No hand but hers could spin the thread and if she span but one skein too few, or one too many, the prince would die at midwinter. The princess rushed to her spinning wheel and worked steadily day after day, but after only a few days she knew she could never spin ten thousand skeins. She burst into tears and her three cats sat by her feet to comfort and console her.

"If you only knew what was wrong I know you'd help me if you could," she said to the three silent white cats at her feet.

To her amazement, one of the three placed its front paws on her knee, stared into the princess's face, opened its mouth and spoke to her: "We know what is needed and we know how to help you," it said. "Cats have no hands, only paws, so we can do the spinning for you and it will not break the terms of the prophecy. Now we must get to work for there is little time left."

And so it was that the three white cats began to spin, each at a wheel provided for it. Each spun rapidly and beautifully. All day the three wheels hummed and when they were silent as evening came the princess looked into the room to find her beloved cats sound asleep next to hundreds of skeins of thread. The days passed and the skeins increased in number. Each time a skein was finished, the prince's health improved and the princess grew more hopeful. On midwinter's eve ten thousand skeins were ready and the prince was almost well.

The gypsy was amazed and pleased at the cats' work though she had been cheated of a life. She told the princess to be sure and show her gratitude to her faithful cats. The princess loved her cats well and wisely and she gave them all her glittering jewels, which they had always loved to play with. On her wedding day, they sat in places of honour on magnificent velvet cushions, each cat with a necklace of precious stones around its neck.

As the feast continued, the three cats curled up contentedly on their cushions and—as cats are wont to do—fell asleep. From all three came loud, contented purring. This was the reward the cats had received for their work. Though no cat would ever again speak, all cats would purr like the whirr and hum of a spinning wheel. From that day to this cats have continued to purr whenever they feel contented.

The Library Cat
Candace Fitts

Excuse me, ma'am. I'm looking for a field guide to butterflies. It's for my son, for a school project. Do you have anything like that?" The patron looked around the library nervously. Her expression was all too familiar to Miriam Caldwell, the reference librarian at the Centerville Public Library. To Miriam, the stacks of books were wonderfully inviting and signaled a world of possibility, but to the uninitiated, she understood that they could be a bit intimidating.

Miriam smiled and nodded. "Of course. We have just the thing for you." The butterfly school project came around once a year at the local elementary school, and Miriam knew the call number for the book by heart. After all, Centerville Public was a very small library, holding just under 15,000 volumes, and Miriam had worked there for thirty years. She knew where nearly everything was.

She walked over to the 595s, pulled the book from the shelf, and then nearly dropped it in shock. There was a ragged hole chewed right through the cover.

Miriam blushed and stammered. "Oh, no, oh dear. I am so sorry. I don't know what's happened here. We'll have to replace it." She shook her head, disgusted, and took the book back to her desk.

"How about this; I'll get the book for you on interlibrary loan. If you'll just give me a little bit of information…"

The next day, Miriam was bemoaning the situation to her friend Jane over lunch at the local meat and three. "Rats, Jane. Rats! In the library! Can you believe it? What am I going to do?"

"What do you mean, what will you do? It's obvious, Miriam. You'll get a library cat."

"Pfff. Nonsense. What's a library cat? I've never heard of such a thing. Is this something you're making up to pawn off one of your strays on me?" Jane ran the Cat Palace, a local shelter that took in strays and unwanted cats and tried to find new owners for them.

"Of course not. Library cats have been around for centuries. They catch the rats, and look after the books. Problem solved."

Miriam had never been a cat lover, herself, and held a few prejudices regarding her friend's preferred species. "I don't know. Don't they spray? What if they shed on the furniture, or chew up the books?"

"Don't be ridiculous. Cats don't chew books; rats do. And as for the spraying, it won't be a problem. All of our cats are fixed as soon as they're old enough. Anyway, I think that I've got just the guy for you."

After lunch, Miriam agreed under much pressure from Jane to go along to the Cat Palace, just for a look. Jane had smiled to herself; it was a rare individual that could go into the shelter just to look and emerge without an animal friend. And Jane knew that despite her friend's posturing, she had a soft heart.

Indeed, an hour later, Miriam emerged from the Cat Palace holding a carrier in one hand and a bag of dry food in the other. Jane followed behind her with a bag of litter and a plastic litter box.

The Library Cat

As they packed everything into the car, Miriam muttered under her breath, "What have I gotten myself talked into?"

Her attitude began to change when she got back to the library to introduce the little cat into his new home. Miriam placed the carrier on the ground and opened the door. From the way the animal had been screeching during the car ride, Miriam expected him to streak out of the carrier at breakneck speed. But nothing happened. The cat did not emerge.

Hesitantly Miriam crouched down onto the ground and looked into the open carrier door. Two gorgeous green eyes peered back at her, wide with fear. Miriam's heart melted a little.

"Aw, come here. Come here, you," she coaxed. Still, the cat did not move. He seemed paralyzed with fright.

Miriam reached a hand into the carrier, letting the cat sniff her as Jane had instructed. He nuzzled his nose against Miriam's palm and took a few steps forward.

"That's it, there we go," said Miriam. Her smile broadened as the cream-colored ball of fur finally crossed the threshold into his new world. He looked around, his eyes now full of what looked like wonder instead of fear.

"Look at you. What on earth are we going to call you?"

According to Jane, the cat had been abandoned, probably when he was young. He was small for his age, probably due to malnutrition as a kitten, and when one of the Cat House workers had found him, his long, light fur had been dirty and matted. "We've been calling him Mickey, but he's yours now, so you can call him whatever you like," Jane had said.

Mickey, Miriam thought, considering. It sounded too flippant for a library cat, not dignified enough. Miriam ran through a list of her own personal literary heroes, looking for one that suited. Salinger? Tom Sawyer? Gandalf? Miriam looked again at the ball of fur, who had found a loose paperclip on the floor and was batting it around in circles, bounding after it when he knocked it out of reach.

All afternoon Miriam watched him settling into his new home, and the librarian couldn't help but be charmed. The cat wanted to play with everything he could get his paws on. Miriam hadn't bought him any toys, but he made do perfectly well on his own, darting under desks and bookshelves to find and retrieve small objects to play with. He found things that Miriam thought had been lost ages ago—her brass letter opener, a crocheted bookmark, a perfect blue marble that Miriam remembered a young boy crying over years before, and which had apparently rolled out of sight beneath the biographies.

"You're quite the little detective," she said. And then she realized what the cat's name should be. "Of course!" she exclaimed. "We'll call you Sherlock!"

That evening as Miriam began to close the library, she found herself hesitating. She had enjoyed Sherlock so much that day that part of her wanted to put him back in the carrier and take him to sleep at her house. He was so small; wouldn't he be afraid by himself in that dark library? Jane had assured her that he would be fine, and that he should get used to living at the library right away. Besides, evening would be prime time for catching rats, which Miriam tried to remind herself was the primary reason for adopting the library cat.

After shutting down the computer, turning off most of the lights, and making sure that the back entrance was locked, Miriam crouched on the ground to say goodnight to Sherlock. "You be brave now. Don't be scared. You'll be a brave little rat catcher, won't you? Yes, I'm sure you will." She rubbed Sherlock's soft chin, lifted him to kiss him on the head, and then exited the library. As she stood outside and locked the glass door, she tried not to look inside at the sweet little ball of fuzz who stood completely still in the middle of the carpeted floor, watching her go with a confused look on his face.

Miriam had checked out several books on cat care before leaving work, and that night she looked at them over a dinner of a peanut butter sandwich and glass of milk. She learned that cats often held grudges when left alone by their owners, and so she was half expecting Sherlock to be upset with her when she went in to the library the next morning. But as soon as she unlocked the door and stepped inside, there he was, rubbing against her ankles and purring.

"Did you miss me?" she asked. She had to admit to herself that she had missed him a little.

Settling in at her desk, Miriam sighed and picked up the chewed butterfly guide that had served the library so well for so many years. "What a shame. Sherlock, I do hope you'll be able to catch the nasty rat that did this. I guess I'd better try to round up some of these chewed books. We'll have to replace them, won't we?"

As she spoke, Miriam realized that this one-sided conversation was one benefit of having a cat. The library could get a little lonely at times, and occasionally Miriam found that hours had passed without her saying a word to another person. But with Sherlock in the room, Miriam could talk as much as she wanted without feeling like a batty old woman.

It was late April, and as the term paper season approached, Miriam had less and less chance to get lonely. Every day brought more students from the local elementary, middle, and high schools, not to mention the occasional overachieving parent who wanted to do the assignment himself or herself to ensure a good grade. During all of this time, Miriam noticed that she was no longer finding evidence of any rats. With Sherlock at her heels, she had spent an entire weekend pulling volumes from the shelves to check for damage, and had rounded up twenty-six books that would need to be replaced. Since then, it seemed to Miriam that no further books had fallen victim to the rats' awful little teeth. Sherlock was doing his job. Miriam rewarded him with all sorts of treats and attention. He spent most of his time during the day curled up on the corner of her desk, purring when she had time to stop by and rub him behind the ears.

The first hint of a new problem came one Saturday in early May, when a teenaged boy asked Miriam to help him find a certain book about baseball cards. He had found the item in the catalog, but he couldn't locate it on the shelf. Miriam remembered the book very well, because it had been expensive, and it had come in just a few weeks before.

"Oh," she said. "That will be shelved with the new nonfiction. That's probably why you couldn't find it."

"Actually, I checked there already," said the young man. Nevertheless, Miriam walked over to the new books, thinking that he'd probably overlooked it. She was astonished to see an empty space on the shelf, right in the spot where she'd remembered putting the book.

"Now that's strange," she muttered under her breath. She walked over to the computer at her desk to see if the book had been checked out, even though she knew that she'd remember if it had been. Sure enough, the book was listed as being there, in the library. Miriam checked all of the library tables and study areas to see if it had just been moved, but she had a sinking feeling, somehow, that the book was gone forever. Lost. She wasn't sure how she knew, but she did.

The Library Cat

Over the next few weeks, similar scenes played out with startling frequency. Miriam came across nearly a dozen missing books, all of which she knew she had seen recently. Was she losing her mind? Had she put the items in the wrong place? When the library was quiet, Miriam browsed the shelves in an attempt to find the missing books, but not a single one of them surfaced.

"What's going on, Sherlock?" she mused one evening as she added yet another title to her list of missing volumes. As obvious as it seemed, Miriam could not bring herself to admit that it might be theft. She couldn't think of a single patron who might be capable of something like that.

Sherlock looked up at her with his thoughtful wide eyes. "Can you help me Sherlock?" Miriam asked. "Can you solve the case?" Miriam sighed. He was just a cat. Of course he couldn't.

The next day was especially busy. As she sat at her desk surveying the patrons and perusing a catalog of office supplies, Miriam mused that many people would be surprised at just how vital a small town library could be. While so many public libraries were suffering from lack of funding and declining membership, Centerville had been an important part of the community for many years. And the current computer craze had only added to the library's use; for many of the people in Centerville, home computers were too expensive to be practical. So if they wanted to check the Internet, they had to come to the library.

And speaking of the Internet, Sherlock took that very moment to spring from Miriam's desk and over to the computer station at the center of the library, startling the librarian out of her reverie. There was a rare empty seat at one of the stations and Sherlock jumped up into it, stretching his paws onto the desk in front of him. The Internet browser was open to a web page. Sherlock raised his paw to the screen, meowing furiously. Miriam had never seen him act this way, and she got up from her desk to see what the commotion was about. When she got to the computer, Miriam couldn't believe what she saw. The open web page was for an online auction business, and the item being sold was the missing book on baseball cards.

"What in the world?" Miriam sat down, hoping that this was just a coincidence. But then she saw that the book was currently for sale, and it was shipping from a Centerville zip code!

She searched the site for another one of the missing book titles, and again, saw a listing that shipped from Centerville. She went and got her list, checked four more books, and each time found one for sale from the Centerville shipper, whose screen name was Dr. Dealgood. Miriam's hands shook with anger. She had not wanted to believe that anyone from Centerville could be stealing the library's books, but now the conclusion was inevitable, and even worse than she imagined. The books were being stolen and sold for profit. And the worst part was that Miriam had no idea who was doing it. Of course, the screen name suggested that it was a male, but that wasn't a certainty, and it didn't narrow things down too much. With a sick feeling in her stomach, Miriam did something that she'd only done one time in her thirty years at the public library; she flipped around the "Open" sign and closed up early.

She spent the rest of the afternoon and the whole evening lying on her couch watching television, which she didn't like to do, finding the activity mind-numbing and boring. Usually, she much preferred to read. But on that particular day, reading reminded her too much of the situation at the library, and brought with it the terrible feeling of betrayal. Of course, it wasn't as if anyone was stealing from Miriam, personally, but that was how it felt. She had always looked at everyone who walked through the library doors as a friend, as someone that she could hopefully help, and one of them had done this awful thing. He'd betrayed not only Miriam, but everyone else who used the library. It made Miriam sick just thinking about it. As she lay on the couch she closed her eyes, wishing that Sherlock was there to sit in her lap and comfort her.

Miriam opened the library reluctantly the next day. She had no plan whatsoever for catching the thief. Of course, she could keep a closer eye on the patrons, but it wouldn't be possible for her to watch everyone all of the time. Miriam had always resisted the idea of getting a security system in the library, thinking that it wasn't necessary. But perhaps times have changed too much, Miriam sighed sadly to herself, shaking her head as she sat down on her desk.

All day, she delivered halfhearted service to the patrons who came and went from Centerville Public Library. She regarded everyone who approached her desk with suspicion, but she didn't see anything too unusual.

That is, unless she counted Sherlock's behavior. The cat didn't usually interact much with people other than Miriam. He preferred sitting on the corner of her desk, or playing with his toys on the floor. But today he was sticking his nose in everyone's business. Miriam had never seen him this way, walking up to strangers and sniffing their shoes, mewing for them to bend down and pet him. "What has gotten into that cat?" she wondered aloud.

At closing time, there were still seven or eight patrons milling about in the stacks and at the computers. "OK, closing time," Miriam called. "Time to go!"

She stood behind her desk, straightening that day's paperwork and waiting for everyone to leave. She was right in the middle of shutting down her computer when she heard an unearthly shriek and looked up to see Sherlock leaping from the top of a bookshelf, through the air, and then landing atop the curly mop of a teenage boy headed for the door.

"Sherlock!" Miriam cried. She ran over to the boy and tried simultaneously to apologize and help him untangle the cat's claws from his hair. But Sherlock wouldn't relent. He held tight to the boy's head, and then shimmied down toward his bulging backpack, which he tore at with his teeth.

Something clicked in Miriam's head. "Son, would you mind opening your pack for just a moment?"

The boy's face went sheet-white, and he began to stutter. "Wh—wh—what for?"

"Just a formality. Sherlock here is our library's unofficial security system, you see, and he wants to see inside your backpack."

The boy shoved the library door open and broke into a run. Sherlock bounded into the parking lot after him, picking up speed. The cat darted between the boy's legs, causing him to trip and dive face first across the parking lot. The overfull backpack flew off of his shoulder and burst open at the zipper. Library books scattered across the parking lot.

Miriam walked over to him and raised an eyebrow. "You've got a lot of explaining to do."

Much to Miriam's relief, it turned out that the boy was not even a cardholder at Centerville Public Library. He'd been driving in from the next county over, and taking the books to sell in his online auctions. Fortunately, he hadn't yet shipped any of the books; the police found the whole lot of them stuffed into a box at the back of his closet. Miriam huffed, thinking of how disgracefully the boy had treated the books, when she heard months later that the boy had received a paltry forty hours of community service for his crimes.

From that day forward, Sherlock became something of a local legend. Patrons starting bringing things from home for him—small toys and cat treats—and Sherlock basked in their attention. Someone even painted a sign for the library, a portrait of Sherlock with the words "Beware of Cat" written beneath it. All of the rats and would-be book thieves heeded the advice.

The Master Cat
or Puss in Boots
Charles Perrault

There was a miller who left no more estate to the three sons he had than his mill, his donkey, and his cat. The partition was soon made. Neither scrivener nor attorney was sent for. They would soon have eaten up all the poor patrimony. The eldest had the mill, the second the donkey, and the youngest nothing but the cat. The poor young fellow was quite comfortless at having so poor a lot.

"My brothers," said he, "may get their living handsomely enough by joining their stocks together; but for my part, when I have eaten up my cat, and made me a muff of his skin, I must die of hunger."

The Cat, who heard all this, but made as if he did not, said to him with a grave and serious air:

"Do not thus afflict yourself, my good master. You have nothing else to do but to give me a bag and get a pair of boots made for me that I may scamper through the dirt and the brambles, and you shall see that you have not so bad a portion in me as you imagine."

The Cat's master did not build very much upon what he said. He had often seen him play a great many cunning tricks to catch rats and mice, as when he used to hang by the heels, or hide himself in the meal, and make as if he were dead; so that he did not altogether despair of his affording him some help in his miserable condition. When the Cat had what he asked for he booted himself very gallantly, and putting his bag about his neck, he held the strings of it in his two forepaws and went into a warren where was great abundance of rabbits. He put bran and sow-thistle into his bag, and stretching out at length, as if he had been dead, he waited for some young rabbits, not yet acquainted with the deceits of the world, to come and rummage his bag for what he had put into it.

Scarce was he lain down but he had what he wanted. A rash and foolish young rabbit jumped into his bag, and Monsieur Puss, immediately drawing close the strings, took and killed him without pity. Proud of his prey, he went with it to the palace and asked to speak with his majesty. He was shown upstairs into the King's apartment, and, making a low reverence, said to him:

"I have brought you, sir, a rabbit of the warren, which my noble lord the Marquis of Carabas" (for that was the title which puss was pleased to give his master) "has commanded me to present to your majesty from him."

"Tell thy master," said the king, "that I thank him and that he does me a great deal of pleasure."

Another time he went and hid himself among some standing corn, holding still his bag open, and when a brace of partridges ran into it he drew the strings and so caught them both. He went and made a present of these to the king, as he had done before of the rabbit which he took in the warren. The king, in like manner, received the partridges with great pleasure, and ordered him some money for drink.

The Cat continued for two or three months thus to carry his Majesty, from time to time, game of his master's taking. One day in particular, when he knew for certain that he was to take the air along the river-side, with his daughter, the most beautiful princess in the world, he said to his master:

"If you will follow my advice your fortune is made. You have nothing else to do but go and wash yourself in the river, in that part I shall show you, and leave the rest to me."

The Marquis of Carabas did what the Cat advised him to, without knowing why or wherefore. While he was washing the King passed by, and the Cat began to cry out:

"Help! Help! My Lord Marquis of Carabas is going to be drowned."

At this noise the King put his head out of the coach-window, and, finding it was the Cat who had so often brought him such good game, he commanded his guards to run immediately to the assistance of his Lordship the Marquis of Carabas. While they were drawing the poor Marquis out of the river, the Cat came up to the coach and told the King that, while his master was washing, there came by some rogues, who went off with his clothes, though he had cried out: "Thieves! Thieves!" several times, as loud as he could.

This cunning Cat had hidden them under a great stone. The King immediately commanded the officers of his wardrobe to run and fetch one of his best suits for the Lord Marquis of Carabas.

The King caressed him after a very extraordinary manner, and as the fine clothes he had given him extremely set off his good mien (for he was well made and very handsome in his person), the King's daughter took a secret inclination to him, and the Marquis of Carabas had no sooner cast two or three respectful and somewhat tender glances but she fell in love with him to distraction. The King would needs have him come into the coach and take part of the airing. The Cat, quite overjoyed to see his project begin to succeed, marched on before, and, meeting with some countrymen, who were mowing a meadow, he said to them:

"Good people, you who are mowing, if you do not tell the King that the meadow you mow belongs to my Lord Marquis of Carabas, you shall be chopped as small as herbs for the pot."

The King did not fail asking of the mowers to whom the meadow they were mowing belonged.

"To my Lord Marquis of Carabas," answered they altogether, for the Cat's threats had made them terribly afraid.

"You see, sir," said the Marquis, "this is a meadow which never fails to yield a plentiful harvest every year."

The Master Cat, who went still on before, met with some reapers, and said to them:

"Good people, you who are reaping, if you do not tell the King that all this corn belongs to the Marquis of Carabas, you shall be chopped as small as herbs for the pot."

The King, who passed by a moment after, would needs know to whom all that corn, which he then saw, did belong.

"To my Lord Marquis of Carabas," replied the reapers, and the King was very well pleased with it, as well as the Marquis, whom he congratulated thereupon. The Master Cat, who went always before, said the same words to all he met, and the King was astonished at the vast estates of my Lord Marquis of Carabas.

Monsieur Puss came at last to a stately castle, the master of which was an ogre, the richest had ever been known; for all the lands which the King had then gone over belonged to this castle. The Cat, who had taken care to inform himself who this ogre was and what he could do, asked to speak with him, saying he could not pass so near his castle without having the honor of paying his respects to him.

The ogre received him as civilly as an ogre could do, and made him sit down.

"I have been assured," said the Cat, "that you have the gift of being able to change yourself into all sorts of creatures you have a mind to; you can, for example, transform yourself into a lion, or elephant, and the like."

"That is true," answered the ogre very briskly; "and to convince you, you shall see me now become a lion."

Puss was so sadly terrified at the sight of a lion so near him that he immediately got into the gutter, not without abundance of trouble and danger, because of his boots, which were of no use at all to him in walking upon the tiles. A little while after, when Puss saw that the ogre had resumed his natural form, he came down, and owned he had been very much frightened.

"I have been, moreover, informed," said the Cat, "but I know not how to believe it, that you have also the power to take on you the shape of the smallest animals; for example, to change yourself into a rat or a mouse; but I must own to you I take this to be impossible."

"Impossible!" cried the ogre; "you shall see that presently."

And at the same time he changed himself into a mouse, and began to run about the floor. Puss no sooner perceived this but he fell upon him and ate him up.

Meanwhile the King, who saw, as he passed, this fine castle of the ogre's, had a mind to go into it. Puss, who heard the noise of his Majesty's coach running over the draw-bridge, ran out, and said to the King:

"Your Majesty is welcome to this castle of my Lord Marquis of Carabas."

"What! My Lord Marquis," cried the King, "and does this castle also belong to you? There can be nothing finer than this court and all the stately buildings which surround it; let us go into it, if you please."

The Marquis gave his hand to the Princess, and followed the King, who went first. They passed into a spacious hall, where they found a magnificent collation, which the ogre had prepared for his friends, who were that very day to visit him, but dared not to enter, knowing the King was there. His Majesty was perfectly charmed with the good qualities of my Lord Marquis of Carabas, as was his daughter, who had fallen violently in love with him, and, seeing the vast estate he possessed, said to him, after having drunk five or six glasses:

"It will be owing to yourself only, my Lord Marquis, if you are not my son-in-law."

The Marquis, making several low bows, accepted the honor which his Majesty conferred upon him, and forthwith, that very same day, married the Princess.

Puss became a great lord, and never ran after mice any more but only for his diversion.

Concerning Cats:
My Own and Some Others
Helen M. Winslow

Chapter I
Concerning the "Pretty Lady"

She was such a Pretty Lady, and gentle withal; so quiet and eminently ladylike in her behavior, and yet dignified and haughtily reserved as a duchess. Still it is better, under certain circumstances, to be a cat than to be a duchess. And no duchess of the realm ever had more faithful retainers or half so abject subjects.

Do not tell me that cats never love people; that only places have real hold upon their affections. The Pretty Lady was contented wherever I, her most humble slave, went with her. She migrated with me from boarding-house to sea-shore cottage; then to regular housekeeping; up to the mountains for a summer, and back home, a long day's journey on the railway; and her attitude was always "Wheresoever thou goest I will go, and thy people shall be my people."

I have known, and loved, and studied many cats, but my knowledge of her alone would convince me that cats love people—in their dignified, reserved way, and when they feel that their love is not wasted; that they reason, and that they seldom act from impulse.

I do not remember that I was born with an inordinate fondness for cats; or that I cried for them as an infant. I do not know, even, that my childhood was marked by an overweening pride in them; this, perhaps, was because my cruel parents established a decree, rigid and unbending as the laws of the Medes and Persians, that we must never have more than one cat at a time. Although this very law may argue that predilection, at an early age, for harboring everything feline which came in my way, which has since become at once a source of comfort and distraction.

After a succession of feline dynasties, the kings and queens of which were handsome, ugly, sleek, forlorn, black, white, deaf, spotted, and otherwise marked, I remember fastening my affections securely upon one kitten who grew up to be the ugliest, gauntest, and dingiest specimen I ever have seen. In the days of his kittenhood I christened him "Tassie" after his mother; but as time sped on, and the name hardly comported with masculine dignity, this was changed to Tacitus, as more befitting his sex. He had a habit of dodging in and out of the front door, which was heavy, and which sometimes swung together before he was well out of it. As a consequence, a caudal appendage with two broken joints was one of his distinguishing features. Besides a broken tail, he had ears which bore the marks of many a hard-fought battle, and an expression which for general "lone and lorn"-ness would have discouraged even Mrs. Gummidge. But I loved him, and judging from the disconsolate and long-continued wailing with which he rilled the house whenever I was away, my affection was not unrequited.

But my real thraldom did not begin until I took the Pretty Lady's mother. We had not been a week in our first house before a handsomely striped tabby, with eyes like beautiful emeralds, who had been the pet and pride of the next-door neighbor for five years, came over and domiciled herself. In due course of time she proudly presented us with five kittens. Educated in the belief that one cat was all that was compatible with respectability, I had four immediately disposed of, keeping the prettiest one, which grew up into the beautiful, fascinating, and seductive maltese "Pretty Lady," with white trimmings to her coat. The mother of Pretty Lady used to catch two mice at a time, and bringing them in together, lay one at my feet and say as plainly as cat language can say, "There, you eat that one, and I'll eat this," and then seem much surprised and disgusted that I had not devoured mine when she had finished her meal.

We were occupying a furnished house for the summer, however, and as we were to board through the winter, I took only the kitten back to town, thinking the mother would return to her former home, just over the fence. But no. For two weeks she refused all food and would not once enter the other house. Then I went out for her, and hearing my voice she came in and sat down before me, literally scolding me for a quarter of an hour. I shall be laughed at, but actual tears stood in her lovely green eyes and ran down her aristocratic nose, attesting her grief and accusing me, louder than her wailing, of perfidy.

I could not keep her. She would not return to her old home. I finally compromised by carrying her in a covered basket a mile and a half and bestowing her upon a friend who loves cats nearly as well as I. But although she was petted, and praised, and fed on the choicest of delicacies, she would not be resigned. After six weeks of mourning, she disappeared, and never was heard of more. Whether she sought a new and more constant mistress, or whether, in her grief at my shameless abandonment of her, she went to some lonely pier and threw herself off the dock, will never be known. But her reproachful gaze and tearful emerald eyes haunted me all winter.

Many a restless night did I have to reproach myself for abandoning a creature who so truly loved me; and in many a dream did she return to heap shame and ignominy upon my repentant head.

This experience determined me to cherish her daughter, whom, rather, I cherished as her son, until there were three little new-born kittens, which in a moment of ignorance I "disposed of" at once. Naturally, the young mother fell exceedingly ill. In the most pathetic way she dragged herself after me, moaning and beseeching for help. Finally, I succumbed, went to a neighbor's where several superfluous kittens had arrived the night before, and begged one. It was a little black fellow, cold and half dead; but the Pretty Lady was beside herself with joy when I bestowed it upon her. For two days she would not leave the box where I established their headquarters, and for months she refused to wean it, or to look upon it as less than absolutely perfect. I may say that the Pretty Lady lived to be nine years old, and had, during that brief period, no less than ninety-three kittens, besides two adopted ones; but never did she bestow upon any of her own offspring that wealth of pride and affection which was showered upon black Bobbie.

When the first child of her adoption was two weeks old, I was ill one morning, and did not appear at breakfast. It had always been her custom to wait for my coming down in the morning, evidently considering it a not unimportant part of her duty to see me well launched for the day. Usually she sat at the head of the stairs and waited patiently until she heard me moving about. Sometimes she came in and sat on a chair at the head of my bed, or gently touched my face with her nose or paw. Although she knew she was at liberty to sleep in my room, she seldom did so, except when she had an infant on her hands. At first she invariably kept him in a lower drawer of my bureau. When he was large enough, she removed him to the foot of the bed, where for a week or two her maternal solicitude and sociable habits of nocturnal conversation with her progeny interfered seriously with my night's rest. If my friends used to notice a wild and haggard appearance of unrest about me at certain periods of the year, the reason stands here confessed.

I was ill when black Bobbie was two weeks old. The Pretty Lady waited until breakfast was over, and as I did not appear, came up and jumped on the bed, where she manifested some curiosity as to my lack of active interest in the world's affairs.

"Now, pussy," I said, putting out my hand and stroking her back, "I'm sick this morning. When you were sick, I went and got you a kitten. Can't you get me one?"

This was all. My sister came in then and spoke to me, and the Pretty Lady left us at once; but in less than two minutes she came back with her cherished kitten in her mouth. Depositing him in my neck, she stood and looked at me, as much as to say:—

"There, you can take him awhile. He cured me and I won't be selfish; I will share him with you."

I was ill for three days, and all that time the kitten was kept with me. When his mother wanted him, she kept him on the foot of the bed, where she nursed, and lapped, and scrubbed him until it seemed as if she must wear even his stolid nerves completely out. But whenever she felt like going out she brought him up and tucked him away in the hollow of my neck, with a little guttural noise that, interpreted, meant:—

"There, now you take care of him awhile. I'm all tired out. Don't wake him up."

But when the infant had dropped soundly asleep, she invariably came back and demanded him; and not only demanded, but dragged him forth from his lair by the nape of the neck, shrieking and protesting, to the foot of the bed again, where he was obliged to go through another course of scrubbing and vigorous maternal attentions that actually kept his fur from growing as fast as the coats of less devotedly cared-for kittens grow.

When I was well enough to leave my room, she transferred him to my lower bureau drawer, and then to a vantage-point behind an old lounge. But she never doubted, apparently, that it was the loan of that kitten that rescued me from an untimely grave.

I have lost many an hour of much-needed sleep from my cat's habit of coming upstairs at four a.m. and jumping suddenly upon the bed; perhaps landing on the pit of my stomach. Waking in that fashion, unsympathetic persons would have pardoned me if I had indulged in injudicious language, or had even thrown the cat violently from my otherwise peaceful couch. But conscience has not to upbraid me with any of these things. I flatter myself that I bear even this patiently; I remember to have often made sleepy but pleasant remarks to the faithful little friend whose affection for me and whose desire to behold my countenance was too great to permit her to wait till breakfast time.

If I lay awake for hours afterward, perhaps getting nothing more than literal "cat-naps," I consoled myself with remembering how Richelieu, and Wellington, and Mohammed, and otherwise great as well as discriminating persons, loved cats; I remembered, with some stirrings of secret pride, that it is only the artistic nature, the truly aesthetic soul that appreciates poetry, and grace, and all refined beauty, who truly loves cats; and thus meditating with closed eyes, I courted slumber again, throughout the breaking dawn, while the cat purred in delight close at hand.

The Pretty Lady was evidently of Angora or coon descent, as her fur was always longer and silkier than that of ordinary cats. She was fond of all the family. When we boarded in Boston, we kept her in a front room, two flights from the ground. Whenever any of us came in the front door, she knew it. No human being could have told, sitting in a closed room in winter, two flights up, the identity of a person coming up the steps and opening the door. But the Pretty Lady, then only six months old, used to rouse from her nap in a big chair, or from the top of a folding bed, jump down, and be at the hall door ready to greet the incomer, before she was halfway up the stairs. The cat never got down for the wrong person, and she never neglected to meet any and every member of our family who might be entering. The irreverent scoffer may call it "instinct," or talk about the "sense of smell." I call it sagacity.

One summer we all went up to the farm in northern Vermont, and decided to take her and her son, "Mr. McGinty," with us. We put them both in a large market-basket and tied the cover securely. On the train Mr. McGinty manifested a desire to get out, and was allowed to do so, a stout cord having been secured to his collar first, and the other end tied to the car seat. He had a delightful journey, once used to the noise and motion of the train. He sat on our laps, curled up on the seat and took naps, or looked out of the windows with evident puzzlement at the way things had suddenly taken to flying; he even made friends with the passengers, and in general amused himself as any other traveler would on an all-day's journey by rail, except that he did not risk his eyesight by reading newspapers. But the Pretty Lady had not traveled for some years, and did not enjoy the trip as well as formerly; on the contrary she curled herself into a round tight ball in one corner of the basket till the journey's end was reached.

Once at the farm she seemed contented as long as I remained with her. There was plenty of milk and cream, and she caught a great many mice. She was far too dainty to eat them, but she had an inherent pleasure in catching mice, just like her more plebeian sisters; and she enjoyed presenting them to Mr. McGinty or me, or some other worthy object of her solicitude.

She was at first afraid of "the big outdoors." The wide, wind-blown spaces, the broad, sunshiny sky, the silence and the roominess of it all, were quite different from her suburban experiences; and the farm animals, too, were in her opinion curiously dangerous objects. Big Dan, the horse, was truly a horrible creature; the rooster was a new and suspicious species of biped, and the bleating calves objects of her direst hatred.

The pig in his pen possessed for her the most horrid fascination. Again and again would she steal out and place herself where she could see that dreadful, strange, pink, fat creature inside his own quarters. She would fix her round eyes widely upon him in blended fear and admiration. If the pig uttered the characteristic grunt of his race, the Pretty Lady at first ran swiftly away; but afterward she used to turn and gaze anxiously at us, as if to say:—

"Do you hear that? Isn't this a truly horrible creature?" and in other ways evince the same sort of surprise that a professor in the Peabody Museum might, were the skeleton of the megatherium suddenly to accost him after the manner peculiar to its kind.

It was funnier, even, to see Mr. McGinty on the morning after his arrival at the farm, as he sallied forth and made acquaintance with other of God's creatures than humans and cats, and the natural enemy of his kind, the dog. In his suburban home he had caught rats and captured on the sly many an English sparrow. When he first investigated his new quarters on the farm, he discovered a beautiful flock of very large birds led by one of truly gorgeous plumage.

"Ah!" thought Mr. McGinty, "this is a great and glorious country, where I can have such birds as these for the catching. Tame, too. I'll have one for breakfast."

So he crouched down, tiger-like, and crept carefully along to a convenient distance and was preparing to spring, when the large and gorgeous bird looked up from his worm and remarked:—

"Cut-cut-cut, ca-dah-cut!" and, taking his wives, withdrew toward the barn.

Mr. McGinty drew back amazed. "This is a queer bird," he seemed to say; "saucy, too. However, I'll soon have him," and he crept more carefully than before up to springing distance, when again this most gorgeous bird drew up and exclaimed, with a note of annoyance:—

"Cut-cut-cut, ca-dah-cut! What ails that old cat, anyway?" And again he led his various wives barn-ward.

Mr. McGinty drew up with a surprised air, and apparently made a cursory study of the leading anatomical features of this strange bird; but he did not like to give up, and soon crouched and prepared for another onslaught. This time Mr. Chanticleer allowed the cat to come up close to his flock, when he turned and remarked in the most amicable manner, "Cut-cut-cut-cut!" which interpreted seemed to mean: "Come now; that's all right. You're evidently new here; but you'd better take my advice and not fool with me."

Anyhow, with this, down went McGinty's hope of a bird breakfast "to the bottom of the sea," and he gave up the hunt. He soon made friends, however, with every animal on the place, and so endeared himself to the owners that he lived out his days there with a hundred acres and more as his own happy hunting-ground.

Not so, the Pretty Lady. I went away on a short visit after a few weeks, leaving her behind. From the moment of my disappearance she was uneasy and unhappy. On the fifth day she disappeared. When I returned and found her not, I am not ashamed to say that I hunted and called her everywhere, nor even that I shed a few tears when days rolled into weeks and she did not appear, as I realized that she might be starving, or have suffered tortures from some larger animal.

There are many remarkable stories of cats who find their way home across almost impossible roads and enormous distances. There is a saying, believed by many people, "You can't lose a cat," which can be proved by hundreds of remarkable returns. But the Pretty Lady had absolutely no sense of locality. She had always lived indoors and had never been allowed to roam the neighborhood. It was five weeks before we found trace of her, and then only by accident. My sister was passing a field of grain, and caught a glimpse of a small creature which she at first thought to be a woodchuck. She turned and looked at it, and called "Pussy, pussy," when with a heart-breaking little cry of utter delight and surprise, our beloved cat came toward her. From the first, the wide expanse of the country had confused her; she had evidently "lost her bearings" and was probably all the time within fifteen minutes' walk of the farm-house.

When found, she was only a shadow of herself, and for the first and only time in her life we could count her ribs. She was wild with delight, and clung to my sister's arms as though fearing to lose her; and in all the fuss that was made over her return, no human being could have showed more affection, or more satisfaction at finding her old friends again.

That she really was lost, and had no sense of locality to guide her home, was proven by her conduct after she returned to her Boston home. I had preceded my sister, and was at the theatre on the evening when she arrived with the Pretty Lady. The latter was carried into the kitchen, taken from her basket, and fed. Then, instead of going around the house and settling herself in her old home, she went into the front hall which she had left four months before, and seated herself on the spot where she always watched and waited when I was out. When I came home at eleven, I saw through the screen door her "that was lost and is found."

She had been waiting to welcome me for three mortal hours.

I wish those people who believe cats have no affection for people could have seen her then. She would not leave me for an instant, and manifested her love in every possible way; and when I retired for the night, she curled up on my pillow and purred herself contentedly to sleep, only rising when I did. After breakfast that first morning after her return, she asked to be let out of the back door, and made me understand that I must go with her. I did so, and she explored every part of the back yard, entreating me in the same way she called her kittens to keep close by her. She investigated our own premises thoroughly and then crept carefully under the fences on either side into the neighbor's precincts where she had formerly visited in friendly fashion; then she came timidly back, all the time keeping watch that she did not lose me. Having finished her tour of inspection, she went in and led me on an investigating trip all through the house, smelling of every corner and base-board, and insisting that every closet door should be opened, so that she might smell each closet through in the same way. When this was done, she settled herself in one of her old nooks for a nap and allowed me to leave.

But never again did she go out of sight of the house. For more than a year she would not go even into a neighbor's yard, and when she finally decided that it might be safe to crawl under the fences on to other territory, she invariably turned about to sit facing the house, as though living up to a firm determination never to lose sight of it again. This practice she kept up until at the close of her last mortal sickness, when she crawled into a dark place under a neighboring barn and said good-by to earthly fears and worries forever.

Requiescat in pace, my Pretty Lady. I wish all your sex had your gentle dignity, and grace, and beauty, to say nothing of your faithfulness and affection. Like Mother Michel's "Monmouth," it may be said of you:—

"She was merely a cat,
But her Sublime Virtues place her on a level with
The Most Celebrated Mortals, and
In Ancient Egypt
Altars would have been Erected to her
Memory."

A Sister for Deuce
Marcia Calhoun

Mary and Dave Keller never planned on having more than one cat. For years, it had been just them and Deuce, and that was how all three of them liked it. They found Deuce when he was a tiny stray kitten in the alley next to their house, and they had raised him into a strong, happy cat who knew he was master of the house.

So when their neighbor Sarah announced over dinner one night that she'd decided to move to France and wanted Mary and Dave to take in her new kitten, they were hesitant, to say the least.

Dave paused, his fork in mid-dive toward his plate of spaghetti.

Mary nearly choked on her salad, then reached quickly for her glass of water.

"I mean, if it's too much to ask, of course you don't have to." The words spilled out of Sarah. She was not the type of neighbor to make requests. In the four years that she'd lived next door to the Kellers, she'd never asked for so much as a cup of sugar. "I could always try to make other arrangements. I mean, there are several shelters around town..." With these last words, Sarah's eyes filled with tears.

Mary covered Sarah's hand with her own. "Oh, honey, please don't cry. We'll work something out." She made desperate eye contact with her husband across the table, and he came to her rescue.

"Of course we will, Sarah," said Dave. "Here's what we'll do. Why don't you bring Daisy by the house tomorrow, and we'll try it out. Just to see how she and Deuce get along."

Sarah's eyes lit up. "Oh, are you sure? That'd mean so much to me. I just don't have anyone else I can ask. You really mean it?"

"Of course we do," said Mary.

From his perch on the television set across the room, Deuce eyed the lot of them with suspicion.

"Absolutely not!" said Dave to Mary as they discussed the matter while getting ready for bed that night. "Deuce would be impossible if we brought another cat into the house. He doesn't even like sharing us with other people. What would he do with a competitor his own size?"

Mary spat toothpaste into the sink, rinsed her brush, and then smiled to check her teeth in the mirror. She turned to look at Dave and nodded. "I couldn't agree with you more."

"Really?" he asked, sliding into the bed and folding the covers back for Mary on her side.

"Really," she said as she got into the bed next to him.

"Well, good. Then we're agreed," Dave said. But each of them had seen Sarah's kitten, Daisy. She was a soft, tiny Siamese with the prettiest blue eyes and the most perfect brown ears. Not to mention that Sarah was one of their dearest friends. So as Mary flipped off the lights and they settled into bed, both of them knew that it would take a major disaster to make them to say no to Sarah and Daisy.

When Mary answered the door the next day Sarah stood there timidly, the tiny kitten tucked beneath her arm. "The carrier really upsets her, and I didn't see the need, since we're just next door."

"Sure," said Mary, though she really would have preferred to let

Deuce sniff out the kitten in the carrier, rather than giving her free reign to run around what he thought was his territory.

"Where's Deuce? Should I just set her down?" asked Sarah.

"Hmm, better hold her for a minute and let him see her with you. Have a seat," Mary said, gesturing toward the couch. "Want anything to drink?"

"Sure, a coke would be great."

Mary went to the kitchen and poured one for her friend and one for herself. When she got back to the den, Deuce had entered the room and was approaching the couch where Sarah sat with Daisy. He jumped up onto the couch, sniffed Daisy, and then turned and walked away, lifting his tail in her general direction. To everyone witnessing the event, it looked like a royal snub.

Sarah sat watching as Deuce strolled casually over toward his bowl. "Well," Mary said quietly, "that went better than I thought it would."

Of course, Daisy stayed. Mary and Dave couldn't stand the thought of her going to a shelter anymore than they could stand the thought of upsetting Sarah. And since there had been no open fighting when the two cats met, Dave and Mary just held their breath and hoped for the best.

The first day, Daisy made it clear that Deuce was no longer the undisputed master of the house. For a few hours she followed around at the older cat's heels forcing him to play with her, though it was obvious that Deuce wanted nothing more than to lie in the sunny windowsill and be left alone. In fact, this is exactly what he was doing when Daisy grabbed hold of his swishing tail and tried to use it as a rope to climb up and join him on the windowsill. In a flash, Deuce was on the ground next to her, hair raised, back arched. Mary and Dave were in the kitchen washing dishes, and they ran to the door to see what all of the hissing was about.

Mary took a step in the cats' direction to break up the fight before it started, but Dave put his arm up and stopped her. "No, they have to work it out on their own. They've got to establish some kind of dynamic with each other," he said. Mary rolled her eyes. Dave taught high school psychology. He was always making her roll her eyes. Still, Mary stayed put and watched to see how the situation played out.

Deuce stood for a moment like a statue, and then to everyone's amazement, including Daisy's, he assumed his normal posture and walked away, unfazed.

"He's really taking the high road, isn't he?" Mary asked Dave. "I wouldn't have expected him to let her get away with so much."

Dave considered this for a while. "I guess it's surprising how getting a baby sister can change a boy."

Mary nodded. "Yeah. I guess it is."

Over the next few days, Daisy didn't let up much on her big brother. She was constantly tormenting him—eating out of his food bowl when her own was empty, pulling at his tail, climbing onto his back as if he might be willing to give her a ride. Deuce responded with apathy and the occasional swat of a paw. He never tried to fight Daisy or even to act out in protest. However, he didn't reciprocate, either. Both Mary and Dave got the distinct impression that if Daisy were to vanish from the face of the earth, it wouldn't bother Deuce much.

And Deuce did have one thing that he could hold over his little sister's head. While he was neutered and allowed to go outside, Daisy was declawed, a confirmed indoor cat. She hated being left behind. Deuce would walk over to the screen door, tap it with his paw, and Mary or Dave would come to unlock it for him. Daisy, however, would be scooped up and held against her will until the door was again locked. Then usually, Deuce would saunter back and forth before the door, just on the other side of the screen, while Daisy mewed in pathetic jealousy. He would look at his adopted sister with haughty eyes, and then make a show of pouncing on a particularly juicy beetle, while helpless Daisy watched on from behind her screened prison.

One hot day, Mary and Dave were both out working in the garden. They'd been at it for hours without a break, trying to pull up weeds and dead roots to get the patch of ground ready for planting, and both of them were ready for a break. Just as they were about to head inside for a glass of lemonade, Deuce sped out of the trees and over to them. He circled quickly around Dave's ankles, mewing with urgency. "Hey Deucey," said Dave, leaning over to pet him. But Deuce didn't want to be petted. He pushed away from Dave's hand, crying like a kitten. "What's the matter, fellah? Are you hungry? Come on. Mom and I are going inside— we'll get you a snack, alright?"

Mary had made her way over to the porch and was just about to push open the screen door when she stopped dead still. "Dave!" she called. "Did you leave the door open?"

Sure enough, the screen door was cracked, and the heavy door behind it hung wide open.

"No, I don't think so," Dave said as he jogged over to her. "Why?"

Mary's voice was high and tight. "Because it's open!"

"Oh, no," said Dave. "Where's Daisy?" Mary didn't hear the question. She was already inside, calling the kitten's name frantically. The two of them tore through the house, looking under beds and atop cabinets. Deuce and his plaintive cries were for the moment forgotten.

But the older cat did not relent. He chased alternately Mary and Dave, his mews gradually sharpening into a screech. "What is it, Deuce?" yelled Mary. Deuce turned and ran outside, looking over his shoulder to make sure Mary was following him. She was.

The Keller's house faced a road, on the far side of which was a deep gully overgrown with vegetation. Deuce stopped at edge of the road to let Mary catch up, and then crossed it. "Deuce, what are you doing?" Mary cried as the cat leapt forward down the steep side of the gully.

"No! Get back here Deuce!" Mary yelled. Now they had two missing cats instead of one. Dave came out of the house and reached Mary just as she was attempting to start down the hill.

"Mary, what are you doing? You can't go down there. You'll break your neck!"

"I have to. Deuce just ran down there. I've got to get him out. There's all kinds of things he could get hurt on down there. Snakes, and foxes, and…" Mary realized that she was crying. Dave put his arms around her and squeezed.

"Shhh, don't worry, we'll figure this out." At that moment, they heard the tiny cries that they'd come to recognize as Daisy's. They were coming from down in the gully.

Dave and Mary looked at each other with startled expressions. "Daisy? Deuce?" Dave called. Even though he'd warned Mary not to just minutes before, he began to wade tremulously down the hill through the thick underbrush.

David didn't get far, though, before they saw something rustling beneath the kudzu just a few feet away. The movement continued toward the road, and there emerged Deuce, carrying Daisy by the scruff of her neck. One of Daisy's legs was bent at a bad angle, and Dave and Mary knew that it was broken.

"Honey, go inside and get a basket and some blankets," yelled

David. "I'll stay here with them." He watched as Deuce gingerly placed the injured kitten down in the grass bordering the road, and then began to lick her wound.

The trip to the vet revealed that Daisy's leg was broken in two places, and she had to have a pin inserted. "You're lucky that Deuce pulled her out," the vet said. "She never could have walked out of there on her own."

When they got back to the house hours later, Deuce, now a hero, was waiting for them. He enjoyed a dinner of canned tuna, his favorite meal.

And perhaps the best part for Deuce was that he got to eat the meal in peace, while Daisy watched on from a padded carrier. Much to the kitten's dismay, the vet had confined her to the small cage until her bones could heal. Deuce did not seem to mind this a bit. In fact, he spent several hours a day walking slowly past the padded cage as his little sister pouted inside it.

Night of the Howling Chipmunk
J.B. Smith

The noise of the cat flap, unusually loud, startled me out of the sofa slumber I was slipping toward. I looked over the back of the couch and saw the swishing, twirling tail of Buttercup, the ebony-colored cat that lives with me, prance through the kitchen. My eyes noticed nothing out of the ordinary, but the second glance afforded me the view of twitching whiskers escaping from the side of her mouth. I bellowed in her direction.

"Drop that creature!"

Her features took on a disdainful appearance, an unspoken phrase sent into my direction. *If you say so.* As if on cue, her jaws parted and a furry, hand-sized thing leaped and landed on the linoleum floor. It skidded to a halt in front of the oven drawer, looked at Buttercup, looked at me and raced through the archway towards the back of the house and an endless supply of hiding places.

Tux, my black and white Labrador, although previously oblivious in sleep, awoke as if the starting gate rose and the rabbit had taken off. He skidded his way through the kitchen, past the watching cat, and through the dining room right on the heels of the animal. I rose and quickly followed, glowered in Buttercup's direction, and I swore that she smiled at me as I passed her. The animal lapped the dining room table with Tux close on its heels, nipping at the short, bushy tail. I stooped and caught the buckle of his collar, almost hitting the clasp, but it managed to hold. I hustled him to the kitchen door and shoved him unceremoniously outside. In my mind the sky had now darkened. The situation would be a little different if this was perhaps the first creature to be dropped off in the house, but alas, no.

As I passed through the kitchen, Buttercup remained in her same state, disdainful and slightly elated, if a cat could be described in such a way. I shut the bi-fold door that separated the kitchen from the rest of the house. Armed with a flashlight and an old straw broom, I began my methodical search of every nook and cranny, under every chair, bed, and table, and around every doorway.

I inadvertently swung the flashlight toward the fireplace in the den and caught a gleam on the mantel. Swinging it back, the beam squared on the brown, furry, shaking thing, hiding in between my wedding pictures and the small pendulum clock. It was definitely a chipmunk, and before I could make a move, it made a suicide leap off the mantel onto the pile carpet. I felt more than saw the ground mammal run between my legs and my too slow broom towards the back of the house and the three bedrooms of my household. From mine and my husband's room came a short squawk and a longer hiss. The chipmunk ran even faster in my direction with Heidi, a brown and white tabby, chasing hardily.

Scooping her up by the scruff of the neck, and momentarily forgetting about the creature, I scolded her sharply. "Don't you dare harm that thing!"

When I glanced around, hoping to catch a fleeting glimpse, the chipmunk was nowhere to be seen. Sighing heavily, I put Heidi inside the kitchen, closed the door and continued to search. Eventually, I gave up the search until my husband came home. He looked through every single room and never found a thing. We decided to go to bed and look again in the morning before going to work.

Peaceful sleep was not only interrupted but shattered into a non-existing dream. Tux sprang with a loud bark from the floor at the foot of the bed, causing my husband and myself to shoot straight from under the covers. Half-doused in sleep, and grumbling like a lumberjack with low pay, my husband stumbled out of the room after the fast-moving hound, shouting his name. I pulled on my robe and followed him, flipping lights on as I went. I passed the dining table on the way to the kitchen and Heidi and Buttercup were sitting side by side, watching both my husband and me pass them by. If I had turned my head, I think I would have seen them high-five each other and swish tails. I walked into the kitchen and looked across to the living room to see Tux snapping at a leaping, sliding, and dodging chipmunk going from furniture to furniture. My husband seemed not to pay attention but put his head down on kitchen counter and moaned upwards at me.

"If we are going to chase that thing, I am going to need a very large pot of coffee."

I ignored him and handed him the broom from the corner while I grabbed the mop. "Open the front door, and I will try to send him in your direction."

As he stumbled to the door, rubbing the sleep from his eyes, he did not even notice the chipmunk run right over his toes but he did notice the dog smash head-long into his leg, causing it to buckle. The broom was dropped and my husband tumbled over the arm of our couch, crying out in surprise. Tux sprinted past me hot on the heels of the escapee. I ran towards the front door to open it, but the duo detoured again towards the back of the house.

Following, I tried to get ahead of them but the chipmunk swerved into the bathroom and dove under the foot board of the cabinet. I sighed loudly, knowing that getting it out from under there was going to be a difficult task to say the least. My husband finally arrived and grabbed the snorting sniffing dog and locked him into the spare bedroom. He did not enjoy that, on the other hand, the cats were still sitting on the dining table and seemed to be thoroughly thrilled at the excitement in their household. Almost as if they had planned the whole thing, and now that the dog was locked away, both Heidi and Buttercup slinked off their perches and came to closely inspect the chaos of their design.

"Those two seem happier than when they are being fed," my husband remarked, clasping the broom and rubbing his leg. If it did not look like he was hurting I would have laughed at him. He stared directly into the cats' faces. "You two are in trouble."

"Buttercup brought it in, Heidi was asleep," I admonished him.

"Maybe, but I think both of them planned this for their own amusement, I can tell."

I snorted as I stuck the mop handle under the cabinet, trying to root out the invader. "Go open the front door, and we will try to hustle it, we might get lucky this will go quickly."

He left with the broom and I heard the door open and there was no sign of the chipmunk in the bathroom. The cats however were still swishing their tails in delight and mewing softly. I was on my knees peering under the cabinet and looked up to see Buttercup leaning forward, staring hungrily toward the ground. Heidi, who moved closer to Buttercup, was leaning in the same direction. As they stared and seemed to gather themselves for a leap, it dawned on me that they were probably looking at the same thing that was crawling over my hand. I looked down and my fingertips were no longer visible but obscured by the chipmunk. I yelped loudly and tried to grab it with my free hand. The animal seemed to squeak and squirmed in my hands and nearly escaped over my thumb.

Everything slowed down and I saw the creature's mouth open wide, revealing razor sharp rows of teeth. I could feel my eyes grow large and the chipmunk's jaws clamped onto my thumb right behind the nail. I screamed long and loud, while the chipmunk jumped down and ran out of the room, blood seemed to gush and squirt everywhere and my head grew light. I heard an elated yelp from direction of the front door, and then it consequently slammed shut.

My husband's face appeared in the doorway, with a grin a mile wide. "Bobby Orr could not have made a better shot than that!" he exclaimed. "That sucker flew out of the door. I should play for the Red Wings!"

Then he stopped and finally noticed me in the corner of the bathroom, curled into the fetal position. "I heard you scream, are you okay?" I moaned in reply and showed him my blood covered thumb, it felt as is if it was hanging off my hand. He looked at it and scrunched his face to look at it closer.

"Oh," he said simply. "I'll get a Band-Aide and some Neosporin, and we will fix that right up." He started to leave the room, but I hadn't moved. "You okay?"

I just glared at him. He looked at the cats, who had returned to their swishing, almost smiling positions.

"I still think those cats brought that thing in here on purpose. It seemed disappointed that it was leaving the house."

He stared at them a little longer until I moaned again. Every now and again those cats bring in an animal or two, but when it is a chipmunk my nearly-severed thumb throbs and I will always remember that very long night.

The Black Cat
Edgar Allan Poe

For the most wild, yet most homely narrative which I am about to pen, I neither expect nor solicit belief. Mad indeed would I be to expect it, in a case where my very senses reject their own evidence. Yet, mad am I not—and very surely do I not dream. But to-morrow I die, and to-day I would unburthen my soul. My immediate purpose is to place before the world, plainly, succinctly, and without comment, a series of mere household events. In their consequences, these events have terrified—have tortured—have destroyed me. Yet I will not attempt to expound them. To me, they have presented little but Horror—to many they will seem less terrible than *barroques*. Hereafter, perhaps, some intellect may be found which will reduce my phantasm to the common-place—some intellect more calm, more logical, and far less excitable than my own, which will perceive, in the circumstances I detail with awe, nothing more than an ordinary succession of very natural causes and effects.

From my infancy I was noted for the docility and humanity of my disposition. My tenderness of heart was even so conspicuous as to make me the jest of my companions. I was especially fond of animals, and was indulged by my parents with a great variety of pets. With these I spent most of my time, and never was so happy as when feeding and caressing them. This peculiarity of character grew with my growth, and in my manhood, I derived from it one of my principal sources of pleasure. To those who have cherished an affection for a faithful and sagacious dog, I need hardly be at the trouble of explaining the nature or the intensity of the gratification thus derivable. There is something in the unselfish and self-sacrificing love of a brute, which goes directly to the heart of him who has had frequent occasion to test the paltry friendship and gossamer fidelity of mere *Man*.

I married early, and was happy to find in my wife a disposition not uncongenial with my own. Observing my partiality for domestic pets, she lost no opportunity of procuring those of the most agreeable kind. We had birds, gold-fish, a fine dog, rabbits, a small monkey, and *a cat*.

This latter was a remarkably large and beautiful animal, entirely black, and sagacious to an astonishing degree. In speaking of his intelligence, my wife, who at heart was not a little tinctured with superstition, made frequent allusion to the ancient popular notion, which regarded all black cats as witches in disguise. Not that she was ever *serious* upon this point—and I mention the matter at all for no better reason than that it happens, just now, to be remembered.

Pluto—this was the cat's name—was my favorite pet and playmate. I alone fed him, and he attended me wherever I went about the house. It was even with difficulty that I could prevent him from following me through the streets.

Our friendship lasted, in this manner, for several years, during which my general temperament and character—through the instrumentality of the Fiend Intemperance—had (I blush to confess it) experienced a radical alteration for the worse. I grew, day by day, more moody, more irritable, more regardless of the feelings of others. I suffered myself to use intemperate language to my wife. At length, I even offered her personal violence. My pets, of course, were made to feel the change in my disposition. I not only neglected, but ill-used them. For Pluto, however, I still retained sufficient regard to restrain me from maltreating him, as I made no scruple of maltreating the rabbits, the monkey, or even the dog, when by accident, or through affection, they came in my way. But my disease grew upon me—for what disease is like Alcohol!—and at length even Pluto, who was now becoming old, and consequently somewhat peevish—even Pluto began to experience the effects of my ill temper.

One night, returning home, much intoxicated, from one of my haunts about town, I fancied that the cat avoided my presence. I seized him; when, in his fright at my violence, he inflicted a slight wound upon my hand with his teeth. The fury of a demon instantly possessed me. I knew myself no longer. My original soul seemed, at once, to take its flight from my body and a more than fiendish malevolence, gin-nurtured, thrilled every fibre of my frame. I took from my waistcoat-pocket a pen-knife, opened it, grasped the poor beast by the throat, and deliberately cut one of its eyes from the socket! I blush, I burn, I shudder, while I pen the damnable atrocity.

When reason returned with the morning—when I had slept off the fumes of the night's debauch—I experienced a sentiment half of horror, half of remorse, for the crime of which I had been guilty; but it was, at best, a feeble and equivocal feeling, and the soul remained untouched. I again plunged into excess, and soon drowned in wine all memory of the deed.

In the meantime the cat slowly recovered. The socket of the lost eye presented, it is true, a frightful appearance, but he no longer appeared to suffer any pain. He went about the house as usual, but, as might be expected, fled in extreme terror at my approach. I had so much of my old heart left, as to be at first grieved by this evident dislike on the part of a creature which had once so loved me. But this feeling soon gave place to irritation. And then came, as if to my final and irrevocable overthrow, the spirit of *perverseness*. Of this spirit philosophy takes no account. Yet I am not more sure that my soul lives, than I am that perverseness is one of the primitive impulses of the human heart—one of the indivisible primary faculties, or sentiments, which give direction to the character of Man. Who has not, a hundred times, found himself committing a vile or a silly action, for no other reason than because he knows he should not? Have we not a perpetual inclination, in the teeth of our best judgment, to violate that which is *Law*, merely because we understand it to be such? This spirit of perverseness, I say, came to my final overthrow. It was this unfathomable longing of the soul *to vex itself*—to offer violence to its own nature—to do wrong for the wrong's sake only—that urged me to continue and finally to consummate the injury I had inflicted upon the unoffending brute. One morning, in cool blood, I slipped a noose about its neck and hung it to the limb of a tree;—hung it with the tears streaming from my eyes, and with the bitterest remorse at my heart; —hung it *because* I knew that it had loved me, and *because* I felt it had given me no reason of offence; —hung it *because* I knew that in so doing I was committing a sin—a deadly sin that would so jeopardize my immortal soul as to place it—if such a thing were possible—even beyond the reach of the infinite mercy of the Most Merciful and Most Terrible God.

On the night of the day on which this cruel deed was done, I was aroused from sleep by the cry of fire. The curtains of my bed were in flames. The whole house was blazing. It was with great difficulty that my wife, a servant, and myself, made our escape from the conflagration. The destruction was complete. My entire worldly wealth was swallowed up, and I resigned myself thenceforward to despair.

I am above the weakness of seeking to establish a sequence of cause and effect, between the disaster and the atrocity. But I am detailing a chain of facts—and wish not to leave even a possible link imperfect. On the day succeeding the fire, I visited the ruins. The walls, with one exception, had fallen in. This exception was found in a compartment wall, not very thick, which stood about the middle of the house, and against which had rested the head of my bed. The plastering had here, in great measure, resisted the action of the fire—a fact which I attributed to its having been recently spread. About this wall a dense crowd were collected, and many persons seemed to be examining a particular portion of it with very minute and eager attention. The words "strange!" "singular!" and other similar expressions, excited my curiosity. I approached and saw, as if graven in *bas relief* upon the white surface, the figure of a gigantic *cat*. The impression was given with an accuracy truly marvellous. There was a rope about the animal's neck.

When I first beheld this apparition—for I could scarcely regard it as less—my wonder and my terror were extreme. But at length reflection came to my aid. The cat, I remembered, had been hung in a garden adjacent to the house. Upon the alarm of fire, this garden had been immediately filled by the crowd—by some one of whom the animal must have been cut from the tree and thrown, through an open window, into my chamber. This had probably been done with the view of arousing me from sleep. The falling of other walls had compressed the victim of my cruelty into the substance of the freshly-spread plaster; the lime of which, with the flames, and the *ammonia* from the carcass, had then accomplished the portraiture as I saw it.

Although I thus readily accounted to my reason, if not altogether to my conscience, for the startling fact just detailed, it did not the less fail to make a deep impression upon my fancy. For months I could not rid myself of the phantasm of the cat; and, during this period, there came back into my spirit a half-sentiment that seemed, but was not, remorse. I went so far as to regret the loss of the animal, and to look about me, among the vile haunts which I now habitually frequented, for another pet of the same species, and of somewhat similar appearance, with which to supply its place.

One night as I sat, half stupified, in a den of more than infamy, my attention was suddenly drawn to some black object, reposing upon the head of one of the immense hogsheads of Gin, or of Rum, which constituted the chief furniture of the apartment. I had been looking steadily at the top of this hogshead for some minutes, and what now caused me surprise was the fact that I had not sooner perceived the object thereupon. I approached it, and touched it with my hand. It was a black cat—a very large one—fully as large as Pluto, and closely resembling him in every respect but one. Pluto had not a white hair upon any portion of his body; but this cat had a large, although indefinite splotch of white, covering nearly the whole region of the breast. Upon my touching him, he immediately arose, purred loudly, rubbed against my hand, and appeared delighted with my notice. This, then, was the very creature of which I was in search. I at once offered to purchase it of the landlord; but this person made no claim to it—knew nothing of it—had never seen it before.

I continued my caresses, and, when I prepared to go home, the animal evinced a disposition to accompany me. I permitted it to do so; occasionally stooping and patting it as I proceeded. When it reached the house it domesticated itself at once, and became immediately a great favorite with my wife.

The Black Cat

For my own part, I soon found a dislike to it arising within me. This was just the reverse of what I had anticipated; but—I know not how or why it was—its evident fondness for myself rather disgusted and annoyed. By slow degrees, these feelings of disgust and annoyance rose into the bitterness of hatred. I avoided the creature; a certain sense of shame, and the remembrance of my former deed of cruelty, preventing me from physically abusing it. I did not, for some weeks, strike, or otherwise violently ill use it; but gradually—very gradually—I came to look upon it with unutterable loathing, and to flee silently from its odious presence, as from the breath of a pestilence.

What added, no doubt, to my hatred of the beast, was the discovery, on the morning after I brought it home, that, like Pluto, it also had been deprived of one of its eyes. This circumstance, however, only endeared it to my wife, who, as I have already said, possessed, in a high degree, that humanity of feeling which had once been my distinguishing trait, and the source of many of my simplest and purest pleasures.

With my aversion to this cat, however, its partiality for myself seemed to increase. It followed my footsteps with a pertinacity which it would be difficult to make the reader comprehend. Whenever I sat, it would crouch beneath my chair, or spring upon my knees, covering me with its loathsome caresses. If I arose to walk it would get between my feet and thus nearly throw me down, or, fastening its long and sharp claws in my dress, clamber, in this manner, to my breast. At such times, although I longed to destroy it with a blow, I was yet withheld from so doing, partly by a memory of my former crime, but chiefly—let me confess it at once—by absolute dread of the beast.

This dread was not exactly a dread of physical evil—and yet I should be at a loss how otherwise to define it. I am almost ashamed to own—yes, even in this felon's cell, I am almost ashamed to own—that the terror and horror with which the animal inspired me, had been heightened by one of the merest chimaeras it would be possible to conceive. My wife had called my attention, more than once, to the character of the mark of white hair, of which I have spoken, and which constituted the sole visible difference between the strange beast and the one I had destroyed. The reader will remember that this mark, although large, had been originally very indefinite; but, by slow degrees—degrees nearly imperceptible, and which for a long time my Reason struggled to reject as fanciful—it had, at length, assumed a rigorous distinctness of outline. It was now the representation of an object that I shudder to name—and for this, above all, I loathed, and dreaded, and would have rid myself of the monster *had I dared*—it was now, I say, the image of a hideous—of a ghastly thing—of the *gallows*!—oh, mournful and terrible engine of Horror and of Crime—of Agony and of Death!

And now was I indeed wretched beyond the wretchedness of mere Humanity. And *a brute beast*—whose fellow I had contemptuously destroyed—*a brute beast* to work out for *me*—for me a man, fashioned in the image of the High God—so much of insufferable wo! Alas! neither by day nor by night knew I the blessing of Rest any more! During the former the creature left me no moment alone; and, in the latter, I started, hourly, from dreams of unutterable fear, to find the hot breath of *the thing* upon my face, and its vast weight—an incarnate Night-Mare that I had no power to shake off—incumbent eternally upon my *heart*!

Beneath the pressure of torments such as these, the feeble remnant of the good within me succumbed. Evil thoughts became my sole intimates—the darkest and most evil of thoughts. The moodiness of my usual temper increased to hatred of all things and of all mankind; while, from the sudden, frequent, and ungovernable outbursts of a fury to which I now blindly abandoned myself, my uncomplaining wife, alas! was the most usual and the most patient of sufferers.

One day she accompanied me, upon some household errand, into the cellar of the old building which our poverty compelled us to inhabit. The cat followed me down the steep stairs, and, nearly throwing me headlong, exasperated me to madness. Uplifting an axe, and forgetting, in my wrath, the childish dread which had hitherto stayed my hand, I aimed a blow at the animal which, of course, would have proved instantly fatal had it descended as I wished. But this blow was arrested by the hand of my wife. Goaded, by the interference, into a rage more than demoniacal, I withdrew my arm from her grasp and buried the axe in her brain. She fell dead upon the spot, without a groan.

This hideous murder accomplished, I set myself forthwith, and with entire deliberation, to the task of concealing the body. I knew that I could not remove it from the house, either by day or by night, without the risk of being observed by the neighbors. Many projects entered my mind. At one period I thought of cutting the corpse into minute fragments, and destroying them by fire. At another, I resolved to dig a grave for it in the floor of the cellar. Again, I deliberated about casting it in the well in the yard—about packing it in a box, as if merchandize, with the usual arrangements, and so getting a porter to take it from the house. Finally I hit upon what I considered a far better expedient than either of these. I determined to wall it up in the cellar—as the monks of the middle ages are recorded to have walled up their victims.

For a purpose such as this the cellar was well adapted. Its walls were loosely constructed, and had lately been plastered throughout with a rough plaster, which the dampness of the atmosphere had prevented from hardening. Moreover, in one of the walls was a projection, caused by a false chimney, or fireplace, that had been filled up, and made to resemble the red of the cellar. I made no doubt that I could readily displace the bricks at this point, insert the corpse, and wall the whole up as before, so that no eye could detect any thing suspicious. And in this calculation I was not deceived. By means of a crow-bar I easily dislodged the bricks, and, having carefully deposited the body against the inner wall, I propped it in that position, while, with little trouble, I re-laid the whole structure as it originally stood. Having procured mortar, sand, and hair, with every possible precaution, I prepared a plaster which could not be distinguished from the old, and with this I very carefully went over the new brickwork. When I had finished, I felt satisfied that all was right. The wall did not present the slightest appearance of having been disturbed. The rubbish on the floor was picked up with the minutest care. I looked around triumphantly, and said to myself—"Here at least, then, my labor has not been in vain."

My next step was to look for the beast which had been the cause of so much wretchedness; for I had, at length, firmly resolved to put it to death. Had I been able to meet with it, at the moment, there could have been no doubt of its fate; but it appeared that the crafty animal had been alarmed at the violence of my previous anger, and forebore to present itself in my present mood. It is impossible to describe, or to imagine, the deep, the blissful sense of relief which the absence of the detested creature occasioned in my bosom. It did not make its appearance during the night - and thus for one night at least, since its introduction into the house, I soundly and tranquilly slept; aye, slept even with the burden of murder upon my soul!

The second and the third day passed, and still my tormentor came not. Once again I breathed as a freeman. The monster, in terror, had fled the premises forever! I should behold it no more! My happiness was supreme! The guilt of my dark deed disturbed me but little. Some few inquiries had been made, but these had been readily answered. Even a search had been instituted—but of course nothing was to be discovered. I looked upon my future felicity as secured.

Upon the fourth day of the assassination, a party of the police came, very unexpectedly, into the house, and proceeded again to make rigorous investigation of the premises. Secure, however, in the inscrutability of my place of concealment, I felt no embarrassment whatever. The officers bade me accompany them in their search. They left no nook or corner unexplored. At length, for the third or fourth time, they descended into the cellar. I quivered not in a muscle. My heart beat calmly as that of one who slumbers in innocence. I walked the cellar from end to end. I folded my arms upon my bosom, and roamed easily to and fro. The police were thoroughly satisfied and prepared to depart. The glee at my heart was too strong to be restrained. I burned to say if but one word, by way of triumph, and to render doubly sure their assurance of my guiltlessness.

"Gentlemen," I said at last, as the party ascended the steps, "I delight to have allayed your suspicions. I wish you all health, and a little more courtesy. By the bye, gentlemen, this - this is a very well constructed house." [In the rabid desire to say something easily, I scarcely knew what I uttered at all.]— "I may say an *excellently* well constructed house. These walls are you going, gentlemen?—these walls are solidly put together;" and here, through the mere phrenzy of bravado, I rapped heavily, with a cane which I held in my hand, upon that very portion of the brick-work behind which stood the corpse of the wife of my bosom.

But may God shield and deliver me from the fangs of the Arch-Fiend! No sooner had the reverberation of my blows sunk into silence, than I was answered by a voice from within the tomb!—by a cry, at first muffled and broken, like the sobbing of a child, and then quickly swelling into one long, loud, and continuous scream, utterly anomalous and inhuman—a howl—a wailing shriek, half of horror and half of triumph, such as might have arisen only out of hell, conjointly from the throats of the dammed in their agony and of the demons that exult in the damnation.

Of my own thoughts it is folly to speak. Swooning, I staggered to the opposite wall. For one instant the party upon the stairs remained motionless, through extremity of terror and of awe. In the next, a dozen stout arms were toiling at the wall. It fell bodily. The corpse, already greatly decayed and clotted with gore, stood erect before the eyes of the spectators. Upon its head, with red extended mouth and solitary eye of fire, sat the hideous beast whose craft had seduced me into murder, and whose informing voice had consigned me to the hangman. I had walled the monster up within the tomb!

The Cat and the Fiddle
L. Frank Baum

THE CAT AND THE FIDDLE

Hey, diddle, diddle,
The cat and the fiddle,
The cow jumped over the moon!
The little dog laughed
To see such sport,
And the dish ran off with the spoon!

Perhaps you think this verse is all nonsense, and that the things it mentions could never have happened; but they did happen, as you will understand when I have explained them all to you clearly.

Little Bobby was the only son of a small farmer who lived out of town upon a country road. Bobby's mother looked after the house and Bobby's father took care of the farm, and Bobby himself, who was not very big, helped them both as much as he was able.

It was lonely upon the farm, especially when his father and mother were both busy at work, but the boy had one way to amuse himself that served to pass many an hour when he would not otherwise have known what to do. He was very fond of music, and his father one day brought him from the town a small fiddle, or violin, which he soon learned to play upon. I don't suppose he was a very fine musician, but the tunes he played pleased himself; as well as his father and mother, and Bobby's fiddle soon became his constant companion.

One day in the warm summer the farmer and his wife determined to drive to the town to sell their butter and eggs and bring back some groceries in exchange for them, and while they were gone Bobby was to be left alone.

"We shall not be back till late in the evening," said his mother, "for the weather is too warm to drive very fast. But I have left you a dish of bread and milk for your supper, and you must be a good boy and amuse yourself with your fiddle until we return."

Bobby promised to be good and look after the house, and then his father and mother climbed into the wagon and drove away to the town.

The boy was not entirely alone, for there was the big black tabby-cat lying upon the floor in the kitchen, and the little yellow dog barking at the wagon as it drove away, and the big moolie-cow lowing in the pasture down by the brook. Animals are often very good company, and Bobby did not feel nearly as lonely as he would had there been no living thing about the house.

Besides he had some work to do in the garden, pulling up the weeds that grew thick in the carrot-bed, and when the last faint sounds of the wheels had died away he went into the garden and began his task.

The little dog went too, for dogs love to be with people and to watch what is going on; and he sat down near Bobby and cocked up his ears and wagged his tail and seemed to take a great interest in the weeding. Once in a while he would rush away to chase a butterfly or bark at a beetle that crawled through the garden, but he always came back to the boy and kept near his side.

By and by the cat, which found it lonely in the big, empty kitchen, now that Bobby's mother was gone, came walking into the garden also, and lay down upon a path in the sunshine and lazily watched the boy at his work. The dog and the cat were good friends, having lived together so long that they did not care to fight each other. To be sure Towser, as the little dog was called, sometimes tried to tease pussy, being himself very mischievous; but when the cat put out her sharp claws and showed her teeth, Towser, like a wise little dog, quickly ran away, and so they managed to get along in a friendly manner.

By the time the carrot-bed was all weeded, the sun was sinking behind the edge of the forest and the new moon rising in the east, and now Bobby began to feel hungry and went into the house for his dish of bread and milk.

"I think I'll take my supper down to the brook," he said to himself, "and sit upon the grassy bank while I eat it. And I 'll take my fiddle, too, and play upon it to pass the time until father and mother come home."

It was a good idea, for down by the brook it was cool and pleasant; so Bobby took his fiddle under his arm and carried his dish of bread and milk down to the bank that sloped to the edge of the brook. It was rather a steep bank, but Bobby sat upon the edge, and placing his fiddle beside him, leaned against a tree and began to eat his supper.

The little dog had followed at his heels, and the cat also came slowly walking after him, and as Bobby ate, they sat one on either side of him and looked earnestly into his face as if they too were hungry. So he threw some of the bread to Towser, who grabbed it eagerly and swallowed it in the twinkling of an eye. And Bobby left some of the milk in the dish for the cat, also, and she came lazily up and drank it in a dainty, sober fashion, and licked both the dish and spoon until you drop of the milk was left.

Then Bobby picked up his fiddle and tuned it and began to play some of the pretty tunes he knew. And while he played he watched the moon rise higher and higher until it was reflected in the smooth, still water of the brook. Indeed, Bobby could not tell which was the plainest to see, the moon in the sky or the moon in the water. The little dog lay quietly on one side of him, and the cat softly purred upon the other, and even the moolie-cow was attracted by the music and wandered near until she was browsing the grass at the edge of the brook.

After a time, when Bobby had played all the tunes he knew, he laid the fiddle down beside him, near to where the cat slept, and then he lay down upon the bank and began to think. It is very hard to think long upon a dreamy summer night without falling asleep, and very soon Bobby's eyes closed and he forgot all about the dog and the cat and the cow and the fiddle, and dreamed he was Jack the Giant Killer and was just about to slay the biggest giant in the world.

And while he dreamed, the cat sat up and yawned and stretched herself; and then began wagging her long tail from side to side and watching the moon that was reflected in the water.

But the fiddle lay just behind her, and as she moved her tail, she drew it between the strings of the fiddle, where it caught fast. Then she gave her tail a jerk and pulled the fiddle against the tree, which made a loud noise. This frightened the cat greatly, and not knowing what was the matter with her tail, she started to run as fast as she could. But still the fiddle clung to her tail, and at every step it bounded along and made such a noise that she screamed with terror. And in her fright she ran straight towards the cow, which, seeing a black streak coming at her, and hearing the racket made by the fiddle, became also frightened and made such a jump to get out of the way that she jumped right across the brook, leaping over the very spot where the moon shone in the water!

Bobby had been awakened by the noise, and opened his eyes in time to see the cow jump; and at first it seemed to him that she had actually jumped over the moon in the sky, instead of the one in the brook.

The dog was delighted at the sudden excitement caused by the cat, and ran barking and dancing along the bank, so that he presently knocked against the dish, and behold! It slid down the bank, carrying the spoon with it, and fell with a splash into the water of the brook.

As soon as Bobby recovered from his surprise he ran after the cat, which had raced to the house, and soon came to where the fiddle lay upon the ground, it having at last dropped from the cat's tail. He examined it carefully, and was glad to find it was not hurt, in spite of its rough usage. And then he had to go across the brook and drive the cow back over the little bridge, and also to roll up his sleeve and reach into the water to recover the dish and the spoon.

Then he went back to the house and lighted a lamp, and sat down to compose a new tune before his father and mother returned.

The cat had recovered from her fright and lay quietly under the stove, and Towser sat upon the floor panting, with his mouth wide open, and looking so comical that Bobby thought he was actually laughing at the whole occurrence.

And these were the words to the tune that Bobby composed that night:

Hey, diddle, diddle,
The cat and the fiddle,
The cow jumped over the moon!
The little dog laughed
To see such sport,
And the dish ran off with the spoon!

Plato: The Story of a Cat
A.S. Downs

One day last summer a large handsome black cat walked gravely up one side of Main Street, crossed, and went half-way down the other. He stopped at a house called The Den, went up the piazza steps, and paused by an open window.

A lady sitting inside saw and spoke to him; but without taking any notice, he put his paws on the sill, looked around the room as if wondering if it would suit him, and finally gazed into her face.

After thinking a minute he went in, and from that hour took his place as an important member of the family. Civil to all, he gives his love only to the lady whom he first saw; and it is odd to see, as he lies by the fire, how he listens to all conversation, but raises his head only when she speaks, and drops it again when she has finished, with a pleased air.

No other person in the house is so wise, for he alone never makes a mistake. The hours he selects for his exercise are the sunniest; the carpets he lies upon the softest, and he knows the moment he enters the room whether his friend will let him lie in her lap, or whether because of her best gown she will have none of him. No one at The Den can tell how he came to be called Plato. It is a fact that he answers to the name, and when asked if so known before he came there, smiles wisely. "What matters it," the smile says, "how I was called, or where I came from, since I am Plato, and am here?"

He dislikes noise, and entirely disapproves sweeping. A broom and dustpan fill him with anxiety, and he seeks the soft cushions of the big lounge; but when these in their turn are beaten and tossed about, he retreats to the study-table. However, as soon as he learned that once a week his favorite room was turned into chaos, he sought another refuge, and refuses to get up that day until noon.

Many were the speculations as to Plato's Christmas present. All were satisfied with a rattan basket just large enough for him to lie in, with a light open canopy, cushions of cardinal chintz, and a cardinal satin bow to which was fastened a lovely card.

It was set down before Plato, and although it is probable it was the first he had ever seen, he showed neither surprise nor curiosity, but looked at it loftily as if such a retreat should have been given him long ago, for could not any discerning person see he was accustomed to luxury? He stepped in carefully and curled himself gracefully upon the soft cushions, the glowing tints of which were very becoming to his sable beauty.

It was soon seen that Plato was very fond of his basket, and was unwilling to share it in the smallest degree. When little Bessie put her doll in, "just to see if cardinal was becoming to her," he looked so stern and walked so fiercely toward them that dolly's heart sank within her, and Bessie said, "Please excuse us, Plato." If balls and toys were carelessly dropped there he would push them out without delay, and if visitors took up the basket to examine it, he would fix his eyes upon them, thinking, "O yes, you would pick pockets or steal the spoons if I did not watch you."

As his conduct can never be predicted, great was the curiosity when one cold afternoon he was noticed walking up the avenue while a miserable yellow kitten dragged herself after him. She was so thin you could count her bones, and she had been so pulled and kicked that there seemed to be nothing of her but length and—dirt.

When Lord Plato chooses, he enters the front doors, but as he waits no man's pleasure, unless it pleases him first, he has a way of getting in on his own account. Upon one of the shed doors is an old-fashioned latch, which by jumping he can reach and lift with his paw. Having opened the door, he pushed his poor yellow straggler in and followed himself. She laid down at once on the floor, and Plato began washing her with his rough tongue, while the lookers-on assisted his hospitality by bringing a saucer of milk. While she ate Plato rested, looking as pleased as if he were her mother at her enjoyment. The luncheon finished, the washing was resumed, and as the waif was now able to help, she soon looked more respectable. But Plato had not finished his work of mercy. He looked at the door leading to the parlor, then at her; and finally bent down tenderly to her little torn ears, as if whispering, but she would not move. Perhaps in all her wretched life she had never been so comfortable, and believed in letting well enough alone. Reason and persuasion alike useless, Plato concluded to try force and, taking her by the back of the neck, carried her through the house and dropped her close to his dainty cherished basket.

Then he appeared a little uncertain what to do. The basket was nice and warm; he was tired and cold; it had been a present to him; the street wanderer was dirty still; and the rug would be a softer bed than she had ever known. Were these his thoughts, and was it selfishness he conquered when at last he lifted the shivering homeless creature into his own beautiful nest?

Peter: A Cat O' One Tail
Charles Morley

Peter, the admirable cat whose brief history I am about to relate, appeared in the world on a terrible winter's night. A fierce snowstorm was raging, the sleet was driving at a terrific rate through the air, and the streets were banked up with snow-drifts. All traffic had been stopped, the roar of London was hushed, and every one who had the merest pretence of a fireside sought it on this memorable occasion. It was a wild night in the city, a wild night in the country, a wild night at sea, and certainly a most unpropitious night for the birth of a cat, an animal which is always associated with home and hearth. The fact remains that Peter was born on the night of one of the most terrible storms on record.

Our chairs were drawn up to the fire, the tea-things were on brew the table, and my mother was just about to try the strength of it, when Ann Tibbits, our faithful and well-tried maid-of-all-work, bounced into the room without knocking at the door. Her cap was all awry, her hair was dishevelled, and she gasped for breath as she addressed herself to my mother thus, in spasms:

"Please—ma'am—the cat has put her kittens—in—your—bonnet!"

Such a breach of discipline had never been known before in

our prim household, where there was a place for everything, and everything had a place.

My mother pushed her spectacles on to her forehead, and, looking severely at Ann, said: "*Which* one, Ann? My summer bonnet, or—my winter bonnet?"

"The one with the fur lining, ma'am."

"And a most comfortable bonnet to live in, I'm sure!" replied my mother sarcastically, as much as to say that she wished all cats had such a choice under the circumstances. "Another cat would have chosen the one with the lace and the violets, out of sheer perverseness. But there—I *knew* I could depend on a cat which had been trained in *my* house."

My mother poured out a cup of tea, betraying no agitation as she dropped two lumps of sugar into the cup—her customary allowance—and helped herself to cream. In a minute or two, however, she took up her knitting, and I noticed that two stitches in succession were dropped, a sure sign that she was perturbed in spirit. Suddenly my mother turned her eyes to the fire.

"*How many*, Ann?" she continued, addressing our faithful servant, who still remained standing at the table awaiting her orders.

"Seven, ma'am."

"*Seven*!" cried my mother. "Seven—it's outrageous. Why, my bonnet wouldn't hold 'em!"

"Three in the bonnet, ma'am, and two in your new m-u-f-f!"

"My new muff!" cried my mother. "I *knew* you were keeping something back." And the stitches dropped fast and furious. "That's only *five*, Ann," she continued, looking up from her work. "Where are the other two? I insist upon knowing."

"In the Alaska tail boa, ma'am," responded Ann, timidly.

Slowly my mother's wrath evaporated, and her features settled down to their ordinary aspect of composure.

"Well," she said, "it might have been worse. She might have put them in my silk dress. But there—it is evident that something must be done. I'm a kind woman, I hope, but I'm not going to be responsible for seven young and tender kittens. Ann Tibbits, England expects every woman to do her duty!"

"All?" asked Ann.

"Four," replied my mother.

"Now?" asked Ann.

"The sooner the better," said my mother.

At this moment a sudden blast shook every window in the house, which seemed to be in momentary danger of a total collapse.

"Not fit to turn a dog out," murmured my mother. "Not fit to turn a dog out. Ugh! how cold it is, and here am I condemning to death four poor little kittens on a night like this—to snatch them away from their warm mother, my muff, and Alaska tail, and dip them in a bucket of ice-cold water. And yet they must go; but, Ann, I've an idea—*warm* the water. They shall leave the world comfortably. They'll never know it."

The faithful, unemotional Ann carried out her instructions. Peter was one of the three kittens which were born in my mother's fur-lined bonnet, and the white marks on his body always remind me of the terrible snowstorm in the midst of which he sounded his first mew.

After several weeks the liberty which our cat Cordelia had taken with my mother's finery was forgotten, and the household had settled down into its usual humdrum routine. Tibbits had made the new arrivals a bed in the little box-room, and the doctor declared that Mrs. Cordelia was doing as well as could be expected. Every morning we had asked the usual question: "How is Cordelia?" "Quite well, thank you." "And the kittens?" "Also quite well." In due course Ann brought the welcome news that the three kittens had opened their eyes, and the kid glove was at once detached from the knocker of the front door. It was on the morning after they had obtained their blessed sight that I was invited by Tibbits to go downstairs and take my choice. I went down, but I could see nothing of the kittens; there was only Cordelia, with tail twisting, eyes aflame, and whiskers bristling, wheeling round and round a number of straw cases in which champagne had once been packed. Lo! one of the cases began to walk. The movement caught Cordelia's eye, and she knocked it over with her paw. A fluffy, chubby kitten, consisting of a black body with a patch of white on it, was revealed. The little one so captivated my fancy that I put him in my pocket, and without more ado took him upstairs, and publicly announced my determination to claim him as my property.

"What shall we name it?" asked my mother.

"Fiz," said one, alluding to the empty champagne cases,—a suggestion which was at once overruled, as we were a temperate family and little given to sparkling liquids. "Pop" was also voted against, not only as being vulgar, but as going to the other extreme, and leading people to suppose that we were extensively addicted to ginger-ale.

"I think, my dears, as Peter was born on a—" My mother's speech was interrupted by an exultant "Cock-a-doodle-do."

"That horrid fowl again!" exclaimed my mother.

The cock in question was the property of a neighbor, and was a most annoying bird. Even my kitten was disturbed by the defiant note. "*M-e-w*?" said he, in a meek interrogative, as much as to say, "What *is* that dreadful noise?"

"Cock-a-doodle-do," cried the bird again.

"Mew," replied the kitten, this time with a note of anger in his voice. "*Cock-a-doodle*," screamed the bird, evidently in a violent temper. "Mew," said the kitten again, in a tone of remonstrance The remaining syllable of his war-cry and the kitten's reply were cut short by my mother, who put her fingers to her ears, and said:

"And the cock crowed thrice. My dears, I have it!"

"What, mother?"

"We'll call him *Peter*." cried the family.

"Peter Gray?"

"Peter Simple?"

"Peter the Great?"

"No," replied my mother, with a humorous twinkle, "Peter the Apostle," pointing to the Family Bible, which was always kept on a little occasional table in a corner of the sitting-room. "And let Peter be a living warning against fibbing, my dears, whether on a small scale or a large one."

A bowl of water was then placed on the table and, having sprinkled a shower upon his devoted back, I as his proprietor, looking at him closely, cried:

"Arise, Peter; obey thy master."

In the middle of my exhortations, however, Cordelia jumped on the table, took little Peter by the scruff of his neck, and carried him back to the nursery.

The day came when I put Peter into the pocket of my overcoat, and took him away to his new home. I had the greatest confidence in him, being a firm believer in the doctrine of heredity. His father I never knew, but his grandfather bore a great reputation for courage, as was indicated on his tombstone, the inscription on which ran as follows:

Here lies LEAR. Aged about 8 years. A Tom Cat killed in single combat with Tom the Templar whilst defending his hearth and home. England expects every cat to do his duty.

His mother Cordelia was of an affectionate nature, caring little for the chase, indifferent to birds (except sparrows), temperate in the matter of fish, timid of dogs, a kind mother, and had never been known to scratch a child. I believed then that there was every possibility of Peter's inheriting the admirable qualities of his relatives. The world into which he was introduced contained a large assortment of curios which I had bought in many a salesroom, such as bits of old oak, bits of armor, bits of china, bits of tapestry, and innumerable odds and ends which had taken my fancy. Picture, then, Peter drinking his milk from a Crown Derby dish which I had placed in a corner between the toes of a gentleman skeleton whom Time had stained a tobacco brown. The Crown Derby dish and the skeleton were, like the rest of my furniture, "bargains." At this period of his life Peter resembled a series of irregular circles, such as a geometrician might have made in an absent moment: two round eyes, one round head, and one round body. I regarded him much as a young mother would her first baby, for he was my first pet. I watched him lest he should get into danger; I conversed with him in a strange jargon, which I called cats' language; I played with him constantly, and introduced him to a black hole behind the skeleton's left heel, which was supposed to be the home of mice. He kept a close watch on the black hole, and one day, which is never to be forgotten, he caught his first mouse. It was a very little one, but it clung to Peter's nose and made it bleed. Regardless of the pain, Peter marched up to me, tail in air, and laid the half-dead mouse at my feet, with a look in his eyes which said plainly enough, "Shades of Caesar! I claim a Triumph, master."

He returned to the black hole again, and mewed piteously for more. Peter was very green, as you will understand, but he soon discovered that mewing kept the mice away, and having taken the lesson to heart, preserved silence for the future. The mouse-hunts occupied but a small portion of Peter's time. He was full of queer pranks, which youth and high spirits suggested to him. He took a delight in tumbling down the stairs; he hid himself in the mouth of a lion whose head was one of my chief treasures; he tilted against a dragon candlestick like a young St. George; he burnt his budding whiskers in an attempt to discover the source of the flame in the wick of the candle. He became, too, a great connoisseur of vases, ornaments, and pictures, sitting before them and examining them for an hour at a time. He was also very much given to voyages of discovery, dark continents having a peculiar fascination for him. Even the lion's mouth had no terror for him. I once produced him from the interior of a brand-new top hat like a conjurer an omelette. Again, we were very much surprised at breakfast on morning to see Peter walk out of a rabbit-pie in which he had secreted himself.

I used to let my canary fly about the room, and Peter chased him. The canary flew to an old helmet on a shelf, and thus baffled Peter. The canary seemed to know this, for when Peter was in the room he always flew to the helmet and sang in peace. If he perched elsewhere there was a chase. The linnet's cage I placed on the window-sill in sunny weather, and Peter took great interest in him. He could not see the musician, but he heard the music, and tried every means he knew to discover its source.

At last he peeped through a little hole at the back of the cage, and when he saw the bird he was quite satisfied, and made no attempt to disturb it.

In the matter of eating and drinking Peter was inclined to

vegetarianism, being fond of beet-root and cabbage, but he soon took to carnal habits, always liking his food to be divided into three portions, consisting of greens, potatoes, and meat. In addition to such food as we gave him he by no means despised any delicacies he could discover on his own account. For instance he cleaned out a pot of glycerine. Having tilted the lid up, he pulled out the pins from a pincushion, but was saved in time; he was curious about a powder-box, and came mewing downstairs a Peter in white; he did not despise the birds out of a hat; he lost his temper when he saw his rival in the looking-glass, and was beside himself with rage when the glass swung round and he saw only a plain board. His most curious experience was his first glimpse of the moon, which he saw from our bit of back garden. He was rooted to the ground with wonder at the amazing sight, and we called him in vain. The only reply was a melancholy, love-stricken mew which went to my heart.

So Peter rejoiced in the days of his youth, and there was no end to his frolics. But do not think for a moment that his education was neglected, especially in the invaluable matters of manners and deportment, both of which are so essential to advancement in life. I taught him to sit at table; to enter a room with grace, and to leave it with dignity. Indeed, I spared no trouble, and Peter became as rigorous as a Chesterfield in the proper observance of all such matters. I can give you no better example of Peter's extensive knowledge of what was right and wrong in the ceremonial side of life than by telling you that when he felt an irrepressible sneeze forming he trotted out of the room and sneezed outside. When Peter played, too, he played gently, and did not disturb his elders by obtrusive attentions. He never required to be told twice to do a thing. Once was enough for

Peter. Then again in the matter of breakages he was as virtuous a kitten as ever lived. I had thirty precious blue china vases on my sideboard, and through this fragile maze Peter always wound in and out without moving a vase. His virtues in this respect were well known to my servants, who never accused Peter of breaking the milk-jug, or the cups and saucers, I can assure you. Like the best of human beings, he had his faults, but upon these it would be impertinent to touch more than lightly.

Peter was partial to Fridays, because Fridays were devoted to cleaning up. If you have ever watched a woman washing the kitchen floor, you will have noticed that she completes one patch before she proceeds with the next, as if she took pride in each patch, regarding it as a picture. It was Peter's delight to sit and watch this domestic operation; and no sooner was the woman's back turned towards a fresh portion of her territory than Peter ran all over the freshly washed patch and impressed it with the seal of his paws, just as an explorer would indicate a great annexation by a series of flags. That was a mere frolic. It was about this time that I discovered Peter's power as a performing cat. I tied a hare's foot to a piece of string and dangled it before Peter's eyes. I hid the hare's foot in strange places. I flung it downstairs. I threw it upstairs. The hare's foot never failed to attract him. We used to roll on the floor together; we played hide-and-seek together. I noticed that he had a habit of lying on his back with his tail out, his head back, and his paws crossed. By degrees I taught him to assume this attitude at the word of command, so that when I said, "Die, Peter!" Peter turned on his back and became rigid until he received permission to live again.

I also taught him to talk in mews at the word of command. I hear some genial critic exclaim that this cannot be true. I decline to argue with any critic that ever lived, and repeat, fearlessly, and in measured terms, that Peter talked to *me*. Of course he would not drop into conversation with the first person who bade him "good-morning," but I assert again that Peter and I held many conversations together by means of the "mew," used with a score of inflections, often delicately shaded, each of which conveyed its meaning to me.

Peter took to reading, too, quite easily, and sat up with eye-glasses on his nose and a paper between his paws. It was, as you may well imagine, a red-letter day with me when Peter said his prayers for the first time; and I was better pleased when he put his little paws up and lifted his eyes up to the ceiling than with any other of his accomplishments, though they were more appreciated by unthinking friends. It was all very well to place a mouse at my feet and thus play to the gallery, but I felt that Peter's thirst for applause might be his ruin.

When the summer came, and the London pavements began to quake with heat, I determined to fly to the country. As delights are doubled when shared with those we care for, I determined to take Peter with me, so I packed him up in a specially constructed travelling aloon of his own, to wit, a flannel-lined basket containing all the necessary comforts for the journey, such as air-holes and feeding-bottles, and off we started in the highest of spirits. Peter found a new world opened to him, and the thousand and one beauties of the country fascinated us both. We were the guests of a burly farmer, who lived in a queer old house, half timber and half brick, with low-ceilinged rooms. The general living-room was the capacious kitchen, which looked mighty picturesque. Oak panels ran half-way up to the ceiling; the pots and pans were ranged neatly in an open cupboard, pleasantly suggestive of good fare and plenty of it. There were flowers in red pots in the windows, and my bedroom was a picture of coolness and cleanliness.

Amid these pleasant surroundings Peter soon made himself very happy, and became a great friend of a cat called Jack, who took him under his charge and showed him the ways of the country. Jack was a favorite on the farm. He was certainly given to roving, and did not always "come home to tea." As a mouser he had few equals in the countryside, and one evening when we were telling stories by the fireside the farmer told me that Jack had despatched no less than four hundred mice from one hay-rick.

Jack was a disciple of Isaak Walton. He would crouch on a mossy knoll by the edge of the river, and sometimes was successful in capturing a small trout. The farmer was himself a great fisherman. Jack was a study while the preparations were in progress, and, all intent, would follow close at his master's heels. He would crouch among the rushes whilst the tackle was being adjusted, and anxiously scan the water as the fly drifted along the surface. He took a keen delight in the sport, and when a fish was negotiating the bait he always purred loudly in anticipation of the feast in prospect. The trout landed and the line re-cast, he would seize his prey, and with stealthy gait slink off with his prize, leaving the old farmer to discover his loss when he might. Together Jack and Peter roamed over the meadow lands, and the poultry-run was an object of great interest to them. Together they fought the rats, and together they would lie in wait for the thrush and the blackbird,—I am happy to say in vain. The farmer told me that in his youth Jack once took up his residence in the hollow of an old oak, where he lived on the furred and feathered game. At last he returned home. For hours he wandered about his old home, fearful of discovery, now crouching amongst the flower-beds, and now flying in terror at the sound of the hall clock. At last he ventured into the kitchen, entering by the window and creeping to the kitchen hearth, where he dozed off to the music of the cricket, to be welcomed like another Prodigal Son.

Alas! these delights were cut short, for Peter and I were soon compelled to pack up our traps and proceed to the seaside for professional purposes. Peter was not fond of the sea. When I took him out yachting he was compelled to call for the steward; and one day when exploring the rocks at low water, gazing with rapture at his own charming face as it was reflected in the glassy surface of a deep pool, an inquiring young lobster nipped his tail, and the shore rang with piteous calls for help. Peter has never cared for the sea since then, and so deeply was the disaster impressed upon him that I have known him reject a choice bit of meat which happened to have a few grains of salt on it. It wafted him back to the ocean, the lobster, and the steward. What powers of imagination were Peter's!

As these memoirs cover a period of seven or eight years, and as space is limited, my readers will kindly consent to take a seat on the convenient carpet of the magician, and be wafted gently to the next station on the road without further question. This is a pleasant byway in suburban London, greatly frequented by organ-grinders, travelling bears, German bands, and peripatetic white mice. This road is always associated in my mind with the mysterious disappearance of Peter. We had often laughed at the odd old lady who lived two doors higher up, for the anxiety which she displayed when any of her pets were missing. It was our turn now.

This same old lady was very fond of her cats, and had nine of them at the time I am writing of. Every morning when the weather was warm, she and her cats would come out and unconsciously form a succession of tableaux for our amusement. A rug was spread out under the pear tree in the middle of the tiny lawn, a great basket-chair was placed in the middle of this rug, and, these preparations having been made, the old lady, who was very stout, and always wore a monster poke bonnet and a shapeless black silk dress, came out, followed by her nine cats, and took possession of the basket-chair. A little maid then appeared with a tray, on which were nine little blue china saucers and a jug of milk. The nine little saucers were ranged in a semicircle, and filled with milk, whereupon the old lady cried out, "Who says breakfast, dearies? Who says breakfast—breakfast?" This invitation was immediately responded to by the nine cats. When they had done the old lady cried, "Who says washee, dearies? Washee, washee, washee?" Whereupon the nine cats sat on their haunches and proceeded to make their toilettes. The requirements of cleanliness having been satisfied, and the nine basins having been taken away by the little maid, the old lady shouted out, "Who says play, dearies? Playee, playee, playee?" holding out her arms, and calling out, "Dido Dums, Dido Dums, come here, deary," when a fine Persian cat jumped on to her right shoulder. "Now Diddles Doddles, Diddles Doddles," and another Persian cat jumped on to her left shoulder. "Tootsy Wootsy," she called once more, and a black cat scrambled up to the crown of the poke bonnet. And one by one they were summoned by some endearing diminutive, until the nine cats had taken possession of every possible coign of vantage which was offered by the old lady's capacious person. There they sat, waving their tails to and fro, evidently very pleased by their mistress's little attentions. Mrs. Mee was not very popular in the neighborhood, except with the milkman and the butcher. The cats'-meat-man, indeed, who supplied various families in our road, positively hated her—so I gathered from our servant,—and had been heard to say *sotto voce* in unguarded moments, "Ha! ha! I'll be revenged." It was not unnatural, as the cats were fed on mutton cutlets and fresh milk, and cats' meat was at a discount. About three weeks before Peter disappeared, Mrs. Mee, in the short space of three or four days, had lost no less than five cats by a violent death, and five little graves had been dug, marked by five little tombstones, and the five dead cats had been laid in their last resting-places by the hands of the old lady herself. A funeral is not generally amusing, but I could not restrain a smile when I saw my eccentric old neighbor follow the remains of her dead pets, which were reverently carried on the tea-tray by the little serving-maid, the old lady herself leading the way, ringing a muffled peal with the dinner-bell, the remaining cats bringing up the rear, pondering over the fate of their dead comrades.

It happened that three of these unfortunate victims had been found my doorstep. I felt very angry with the old lady, who blamed me for the destruction of her pets, adducing the fact that they were found dying on my doorsteps as proof conclusive. One morning I received an anonymous postcard. Although it bore the Charing Cross postmark, I felt sure it came from the old lady. It read as follows:

The Assyrian came down like a wolf on the fold.

This was the last straw, for I felt that as regards the old lady's cats I had behaved in a sympathetic and neighborly spirit. I remember this post-card because the same afternoon that it came Peter disappeared, and I began to fear that he had yielded to the temptation of a poisoned pig's foot which had been found in my garden stripped of its flesh. This was a delicacy which Peter had never been able to resist, though why he should have preferred it to the choice foods that were daily piled upon his plate I cannot for the life of me say. We searched the neighborhood in vain, and at last I determined to advertise. Accordingly I addressed an advertisement to my favorite paper. It ran as follows:

Come back, Peter. Lost, stolen, strayed, or poisoned, a white and black cat called Peter, who left his friends at— on Monday afternoon last. Round his neck he wore a blue ribbon with the word *Peter* embroidered upon it in red silk. Before retiring to rest he always says his prayers. Dead or alive, a reward of Two Pounds is offered to any one who will restore him to his mourning friends.

I little knew what I was bringing on my devoted head. I had been troubled enough before with dying cats, but now they were all alive. Cats were brought to me in baskets, in boxes, in arms; Manx cats and cats whose tails were missing for other than hereditary reasons; lame cats, blind cats, cats with one eye, and cats who squinted. Never before had I seen such an extraordinary collection. My whole time was now taken up in interviewing callers with cats.

If the boys were bad before, they were a thousand times worse now. Here is one example out of a score. He was a boy known as Pop, who carried the laundry baskets.

"'Ave yer found yer cat yet?"

"No, we haven't."

"Did yer say it was a yaller 'un?"

"No, I didn't."

"What did I say, Hop?" continued Pop, triumphantly turning to a one-legged friend who swept a crossing close by.

"Yer said, Pop, as it was a tortus," murmured the bashful Hop, who had sheltered himself behind Pop.

"A tortus, that's it. A tortus, and Hop and I's found it, sir. We've got it here."

"You're wrong. My cat's *not* a tortoise," I replied. "Bless you, we know that, guv'nor. Just as if we didn't know Peter!

Ah! Peter was a cat as wants a lot of replacin', Peter does. But me and Hop's got a tortus as is a wunner, guv'nor. A heap better nor Peter. Poor old Peter! he's dead and gone. Be sure of that. This 'ere's a reg'lar bad road. A prize-winner, warn't 'e, Hoppy?" They held up the prize-winner, who was *not* a tortoise, and was mangy.

"Look here, my boys, you can take her away. Now, be off. Quick march!"

"Yer don't want it, guv'nor. Jest think agin. Why, 'ow will you get along without a cat? The mice is 'orrible in this 'ere road. Come, guv'nor, I'll tell you what I'll do. You shall 'ave a bargain," said Pop.

I insisted that the tortoise prize-winner should be taken away, and the next day I stopped the advertisement and resigned myself to despair. A week after Peter had disappeared I heard the voice of my friend Pop at the door. "I say, mister, I've some noose. Come along o' me. I think I've found 'im. Real. A blue ribbon round 'is neck and says 'is prayers. Put on yer 'at and foller, foller, foller me." Mr. Pop led the way along the road, and turned off to the right, and we walked up another road until we reached a large house which had been unoccupied for many months. The drains were up, and two or three workmen were busy. Pop at once introduced me as "the gent as was lookin' for his cat." "Have you seen a cat with a blue ribbon round his neck?" I asked them, very dubious as to the honesty of Pop's intention. "Well, sich a cat *'as* bin 'ere for some days," replied the workman to whom I had spoken. "He used to come when we were gettin' our bit of dinner. But we never know'd but wot it came from next door. You go upstairs to the first-floor front, and you'll see a sight." On the top of the stairs was Peter, who knew me at once, and began to purr and rub himself against my legs in a most affectionate manner, as if to appease any outburst of wrath on my part. I felt too pleased to be angry, and followed Peter into the empty room, which was littered with paper and rubbish, and the remains of forty or fifty mice lay strewn about the floor. Peter looked up to me as if to say: "Not a bad bag—eh, master?" In the corner of the room was a bit of sacking which Peter had used as a bed. Pop explained to me that he had heard the men talking about the funny cat that came and dined with them every day. This conversation induced him to search the house, with the happy result that Peter was restored to the bosom of his sorrowing family, and Pop gave up the laundry basket, and invested the reward in a small private business of his own.

Peter and I have had many homes in London and in the country. Together we have lived in flats, in hotels, in farm-houses, and in lodgings for single gentlemen. In lodgings for single gentlemen we had many strange experiences which would occupy too much time to relate, and I will therefore touch but lightly upon this period of Peter's career. Peter, being a gentlemanly cat, never quarreled with ladies, however hard they might be to please, and let them gird at him as they would. For did not that gracious animal, when Mrs. Nagsby was accusing him of stealing fowls, say—did he not march his bonny back and purr against Mrs. Nagsby's ankles and endeavor to appease her? In her softer moods she did sometimes relax, and even allowed Peter to sit by her side as she read the paper. Peter was held responsible for every article that was lost in Mrs. Nagsby's apartments, and the amount of money I paid to that good lady for breakage in the course of six months would have furnished a small cottage. Mrs. Nagsby was a widow, and the late lamented Nagsby had supported her by his performances on the euphonium. This instrument was kept in a case in Mrs. Nagsby's little room, which was on the ground-floor back, and looked on to a series of dingy walls. Mrs. Nagsby used to polish up the euphonium every Saturday morning with a regularity which nothing prevented. Did it not speak volumes for her affection for the late lamented? On one of these Saturdays it happened that a German band stopped a the front door. Mrs. Nagsby could never resist the seductive power of brass music. She rushed upstairs to the first-floor front to listen to the performance. Fate ordained it that Mrs. Nagsby should leave the precious euphonium on the floor in her haste to hear the band. Fate ordained it also that Peter should come down stairs at this particular moment and wend his way to Mrs. Nagsby's parlor. Fate also had ordained it that a mouse which lived in a hole behind Mrs. Nagsby's easy-chair should issue at this particular moment for a little bread-crumb expedition. Mrs. Nagsby was a careful housekeeper, and finding no crumbs about, the mouse roamed into the silent highway presented by the orifice of the euphonium. It was natural enough that Peter should follow the mouse. Unfortunately, Peter's progress was stopped, the girth of his body being too great to admit him; and my door being open, I at once rushed to the rescue, and found Peter with his head in the depths of the euphonium, and making fierce struggles to vacate the position. Mrs. Nagsby came downstairs and entered her parlor just as I succeeded in extracting Peter from the musical instrument. Fiercely was I reproached for Peter's escapade, and humbly did I make his apologies, little knowing the secret of the plight from which I had rescued him. Having soothed my landlady, she at length took up the euphonium and proceeded to apply her eye to the main orifice to see if Peter had damaged it, handling the euphonium in the manner of a telescope. I was thinking of the reproaches in prospect, when I was startled by a loud shriek, to which the euphonium imparted a metallic vibration, and Mrs. Nagsby dropped the instrument on to the floor, the good lady herself following it with a thud. A we mouse scuttled across her face, disappeared behind the easy chair, and doubtless rejoined his anxious family. Mrs. Nagsby recovered after her maid-of-all-work and I had burnt a few sheets of brown paper under her nostrils; but I had great difficulty in making the peace.

In vain I pointed out that the responsibility did not remain with me, or even with Peter. We agreed after some debate that it was the German band, which was never afterwards patronized by Mrs. Nagsby.

I got into further trouble with Mrs. Nagsby owing to a greyhound which I had bought at a sale. I had no character with him, for he had no character. If Mrs. Nagsby had killed him with the meat hatchet I would have held my peace, for never a day passed but King Arthur took his name in vain. The first night I brought him home Mrs. Nagsby gave me permission as a great favor to chain him to the kitchen table. In the morning two of the table legs had been mangled, and that is our reason why I called him King Arthur, of the Round Table. The next night King Arthur was taken upstairs and attached to the leg of my wash-stand. I was awakened out of my beauty sleep by a horrible clamor which caused me to think that the house had fallen in. I presently realized that King Arthur had mistaken the water-jug for a dragon. In any case it was smashed to bits, and the noise brought Mrs. Nagsby to my door in anger. I should be sorry to say what King Arthur cost me in hard cash for breakages and legs of mutton. Poor Peter! thou wast a saint when compared with that fiend on four legs.

The denouement came at last, and it arose from King Arthur's fondness for the ladies. There was nothing remarkable in the appearance of the old lady who was Mrs. Nagsby's favorite lodger, who had held the rooms above mine for three years. But the lady had a most beautiful sealskin jacket, trimmed with tails of sable. King Arthur had unluckily a feminine affection for furs, and I never dared to take him into any of the fashionable thoroughfares, as he had a way of following the ladies, not for their own dear sakes, but for the fur which they might happen to be wearing. Whether they were only tippets or dyed rabbit-skins, it did not matter to King Arthur.

Well, one unfortunate afternoon, I was leading my greyhound home. A few yards in front of us was Mrs. Nagsby's first-floor lady, takin the sun in all the glories of her sealskin jacket and sable tails. To my horror I dropped the chain in taking a match-box out of my pocket, and before I could take any steps to prevent him— *King Arthur was coursing Mrs. Nagsby's first-floor lodger at his highest rate of speed!!!* King Arthur held on his course and literally took the old lady aback, and began to tear those choice sable tippets asunder. Nor was the base creature content to rest at the sable tippets. Before I reached his victim his mouth was full of sealskin. Let me pass on, merely saying that King Arthur was shot that night in the mews at the back of Mrs. Nagsby's, a victim to is own indiscretions.

And now I come to the fatal catastrophe which finally drove me and Peter from the shelter of Mrs. Nagsby's roof. That lady had a set of false teeth which she was in the habit of depositing on her dressing-table when she went to bed. I had learned this from Sara when that damsel was in a confidential mood. Peter, I think I have told you, slept in my room. One very warm night Mrs. Nagsby left her door open, and her night light was burning as usual. I also slept with my door open, and Peter, being hot like the rest of us, left the room for a stroll, and visited Mrs. Nagsby's apartment. Presently he came back with Mrs. Nagsby's teeth between his own—at least I suppose so, for I found them on the hearth-rug when I awoke. I was greatly amused, though a little puzzled to know how I could replace them. After some reflection I went down to breakfast, placed the trophy in a saucer, and showed it to Sarah, who screamed and traitorously ran up and informed her mistress. Mrs. Nagsby came down rampant, but of course speechless. I was thankful for this; but the violent woman, after sputtering spasmodically, caught sight of the missing article in the saucer, and, lost to all sense of shame, replaced it in position and poured forth a torrent of the most violent abuse.

Peter and I left.

The Tale of Tom Kitten
Beatrix Potter

Once upon a time there were three little kittens, and their names were Mittens, Tom Kitten, and Moppet.

They had dear little fur coats of their own; and they tumbled about the doorstep and played in the dust.

But one day their mother—Mrs. Tabitha Twitchit—expected friends to tea; so she fetched the kittens indoors, to wash and dress them, before the fine company arrived.

First she scrubbed their faces (this one is Moppet).

Then she brushed their fur, (this one is Mittens).

Then she combed their tails and whiskers (this is Tom Kitten).

Tom was very naughty, and he scratched.

Mrs. Tabitha dressed Moppet and Mittens in clean pinafores and tuckers; and then she took all sorts of elegant uncomfortable clothes out of a chest of drawers, in order to dress up her son Thomas.

Tom Kitten was very fat, and he had grown; several buttons burst off. His mother sewed them on again.

When the three kittens were ready, Mrs. Tabitha unwisely turned them out into the garden, to be out of the way while she made hot buttered toast.

"Now keep your frocks clean, children! You must walk on your hind legs. Keep away from the dirty ash-pit, and from Sally Henny Penny, and from the pig-stye and the Puddle-Ducks."

Moppet and Mittens walked down the garden path unsteadily. Presently they trod upon their pinafores and fell on their noses.

When they stood up there were several green smears!

"Let us climb up the rockery, and sit on the garden wall," said Moppet.

They turned their pinafores back to front, and went up with a skip and a jump; Moppet's white tucker fell down into the road.

Tom Kitten was quite unable to jump when walking upon his hind legs in trousers. He came up the rockery by degrees, breaking the ferns, and shedding buttons right and left.

He was all in pieces when he reached the top of the wall.

Moppet and Mittens tried to pull him together; his hat fell off, and the rest of his buttons burst.

While they were in difficulties, there was a pit pat paddle pat! and the three Puddle-Ducks came along the hard high road, marching one behind the other and doing the goose step—pit pat paddle pat! pit pat waddle pat!

They stopped and stood in a row, and stared up at the kittens. They had very small eyes and looked surprised.

Then the two duck-birds, Rebeccah and Jemima Puddle-Duck, picked up the hat and tucker and put them on.

Mittens laughed so that she fell off the wall. Moppet and Tom descended after her; the pinafores and all the rest of Tom's clothes came off on the way down.

"Come! Mr. Drake Puddle-Duck," said Moppet—"Come and help us to dress him! Come and button up Tom!"

Mr. Drake Puddle-Duck advanced in a slow sideways manner, and picked up the various articles.

But he put them on *himself*! They fitted him even worse than Tom Kitten.

"It's a very fine morning!" said Mr. Drake Puddle-Duck.

And he and Jemima and Rebeccah Puddle-Duck set off up the road, keeping step—pit pat, paddle pat! pit pat, waddle pat!

Then Tabitha Twitchit came down the garden and found her kittens on the wall with no clothes on.

She pulled them off the wall, smacked them, and took them back to the house.

"My friends will arrive in a minute, and you are not fit to be seen; I am affronted," said Mrs. Tabitha Twitchit.

She sent them upstairs; and I am sorry to say she told her friends that they were in bed with the measles; which was not true.

Quite the contrary; they were not in bed: *not* in the least.

Somehow there were very extraordinary noises over-head, which disturbed the dignity and repose of the tea party.

And I think that some day I shall have to make another, larger, book, to tell you more about Tom Kitten!

As for the Puddle-Ducks—they went into a pond.

The clothes all came off directly, because there were no buttons.

And Mr. Drake Puddle-Duck, and Jemima and Rebeccah, have been looking for them ever since.

Mouser Cats' Story
Amy Prentice

On that day last week when it stormed so very hard, your Aunt Amy was feeling very lonely, because all of her men and women friends in the house were busy, and it was not reasonable to suppose any of her bird or animal acquaintances would be out. As she sat by the window, watching the little streams of water as they ran down the glass, she said to herself that this was one of the days when she could not hope to be entertained by story-telling.

"You don't seem to care whether Mrs. Man makes the pickles properly, or not," a voice from the doorway said, and, looking around in surprise, your Aunt Amy saw Mrs. Mouser Cat, an animal with whom she was very well acquainted, but who had never before ventured to speak with her.

Considerably astonished, because it had not come into her mind that Mrs. Mouser might prove to be as entertaining as any of the other animals she had talked with, your Aunt Amy asked:

"What about the pickles, Mrs. Mouser?"

"Why, Mrs. Man is putting them up; didn't you know it?" the cat replied, and your Aunt Amy said with a sigh:

"Oh, yes indeed, Mrs. Mouser, I know that, and you also know it is not possible for me to do any work around the house, owing to my illness. That is why I am idle on this day when the storm makes it seem very, very lonely.

"You can sit out of doors all the afternoon with a foolish old duck, or talk by the hour with Mr. Turtle, who hasn't got sense enough to go in when it rains, and yet you never invited me for an afternoon's story-telling," and Mrs. Mouser arched her back as if she was angry.

"Do you know any stories?" your Aunt Amy asked, surprised again, and Mrs. Mouser replied quickly:

"It would be funny if I didn't. I've lived on this farm more than six years, and have known pretty much all that has happened around here in that time."

Why Cats Catch Mice

"I wish you could think of a story to tell me now," your Aunt Amy said. "I am just in the mood for hearing one."

"It is the hardest thing in the world to stand up and begin telling a story without anything to start one going," Mrs. Mouser said thoughtfully, as she brushed her whiskers with her paw. "After you once get into it, of course, they come easy enough. How would it do if I should explain why it is that cats catch mice?"

"Was there ever a time when they didn't catch mice?" your Aunt Amy asked, surprised for the third time.

"Oh, yes indeed," Mrs. Mouser said in a matter-of-fact tone. "All cats used to be good friends with the mice, once upon a time, and it happened that because an old Mrs. Pussy, who lived in the city, didn't have anything in the house to eat, the cats took up catching mice. You see it was in this way: A cat that had always lived in the country, made up her mind one day to go and see her cousin in the city, so she put on her bonnet and shawl, wrapped some fried fish in a paper, and started.

"When she got there her cousin saw the fish, and it made her ashamed because she hadn't anything in the house to offer the visitor, so she asked, turning up her nose considerably:

'Do you cats in the country eat fish?' and Mrs. Pussy replied:

'Why, yes, of course we do; don't you?'

'Certainly not; it is thought to be a sign of ill-breeding to eat such vulgar food,' and then remembering that she could not offer her cousin the least little thing, she said, never stopping to think very much about it. We eat mice here. They are delicious; you would be surprised to know what a delicate flavor they have.'

"That surprised the country cousin, and nothing would do but that she must go right out hunting for mice. Of course some one had to go with her, and then it was that the city cat found she hadn't made any such a very great mistake after all, for mice or rats, take them any way you please, cooked or raw, are very nice indeed."

The Kitty Which the Snow Brought

"Do you think that is a true story?" your Aunt Amy asked, and Mrs. Mouser replied:

"I can't really say; but I think it is as true as that the snow brought a white cat to Dolly Man." Your Aunt Amy knew Miss Dolly's kitten very well; but she had never heard any such thing as Mrs. Mouser intimated, therefore, as a matter of course, she was curious regarding the affair, and asked that it be explained to her.

"I was in the house when this happened, so there is no mistake about the story part of it," Mrs. Mouser began. "It was snowing one day, and Dolly, standing by the window, said to her mother that she wished the snow-flakes would turn into a pretty, little, white kitten, so she could have something to play with. She hadn't hardly more than spoken, when they heard a cat calling from out of doors, and

Dolly ran into the hallway, believing the snow-flakes had really turned into a pet for her. Now it is kind of odd, but true just the same, that when she opened the door there stood a white kitten, the same one we call Kitty Snow.

"She was the forlornest little stray kitten you could ever imagine, and as white then as she is now, from her nose to the tip of her tail, but so nearly frozen when Dolly took her in, that they had to wrap her in a blanket, and keep her near the fire two or three hours before she thawed out."

"I believe that you and Kitty Snow are not very good friends," your Aunt Amy said.

"Well, I can't say that we are," Mrs. Mouser replied thoughtfully. "That white cat has been petted so much that she really isn't of any very great service about the house. I don't believe she has caught a mouse in six months, and yet I heard her tell Mr. Towser Dog no longer ago than yesterday, that she was of more value around this farm than I. Just think of it! And it has been proven that I have a good deal more sense than Mr. Fox, cunning as he thinks he is."

When Mr. Fox Was Foolish

As a matter of course, your Aunt Amy asked her what she meant, and Mrs. Mouser sat down at one side of the fireplace, as if making ready for an afternoon of story-telling.

"It was like this," she said. "I was down in the meadow looking for field mice one day, and met Mr. Fox. You know some animals think that he and I are relations; but whether we are or not, we have always been good friends. So he sat down for a chat, and we talked of first this thing and then that, until finally I said, just to make myself agreeable:

"'Do you know, Mr. Fox, I think you are very smart.'

"Well now, would you believe it, that puffed him way up with pride, and he said, grinning in a way that was enough to make any cat laugh:

"'Indeed I am, Mrs. Mouser. There isn't an animal around here who can hold a candle to me for smartness.'

"'What about the dogs?' I asked, thinking to joke him a little, and he turned up his nose as he said:

"'I don't give a snap of my claws for all the dogs there are around this place! Even if four or five of them should come right up here this minute, it wouldn't bother me any. You may not think it; but Mr. Towser is actually afraid of me.'

"Well now, do you know that made me laugh again, because in the first place I knew it wasn't true; but what was the use of saying anything of the kind to him? He was swelled way out with pride, so I changed the conversation, and began talking about mice, when suddenly there was a terrible commotion down the lane, and up came Mr. Towser, Miss Spaniel, and four or five other dogs, barking, and yelping.

"Oh me, oh my, how frightened I was! Up a tree I scurried as fast as my legs would carry me, and not until I was safe on the highest limb did I look around to see Mr. Fox, who didn't care the snap of his claws for dogs; but, bless you, he was going toward the meadow with his tail hanging straight out behind him, while the dogs were gaining on him at every jump. Mr. Towser told me afterward that they made Mr. Fox just about as sick as Mrs. Toad made the bugs."

"What was it Mrs. Toad did?" your Aunt Amy asked, and Mrs. Mouser replied with a grin:

"Perhaps you never heard that Mr. Crow is a great hand at making poetry?"

"I have indeed," your Aunt Amy replied, and it was only with difficulty she prevented herself from laughing aloud. "I have heard of his poetry from every bird and animal around this farm."

A Wet-Weather Party

"Then perhaps you don't care to hear any more?" Mrs. Mouser said inquiringly.

"Indeed I do," your Aunt Amy replied, "if it is anything new, and I surely have never heard of a wet-weather party."

Mrs. Mouser stroked her whiskers a moment, and then began to repeat the following:

A little Black Ant was journeying home
    From a marketing visit to town,
When down came the ram, pitter-patter, so fast,
    It threatened to spoil her best gown.

She wandered about till she quite lost her way,
    Till at last a big Toadstool she found,
"Ah, here I can rest!" said the little Black Ant,
    And she wearily sank to the ground.

And as she sat resting, a light she espied,
    And a Glow-worm came twinkling by.
"Dear me!" exclaimed he, with a gasp and a sob,
    "I don't think I'll ever be dry!"

"Come in, sir, come in," said the little Black Ant,
    "Here is plenty of room, sir, for two.
Pray bring in your light, sir, and sit down by me,
    Or else you'll be surely wet through."

The Glow-worm agreed, and soon brought in his light,
    When a cricket appeared on the scene
With her fiddle and bow (she's a minstrel, you know)
    —To a concert in town she had been.

"Come in, ma'am, come in!" said the little Black Ant,
    "Here is shelter and light for us all!
And if you could play us a nice little tune,
    We might fancy we were at a ball."

"Hear, hear!" said the voice of the Stag-Beetle bold,
    Who just then was passing that way;
"And if there is dancing, I hope, dear Miss Ant,
    That you will allow *me* to stay!"

"Come in, sir, come in!" said the little Black Ant,
    "The more, sir, the merrier we!
And here, I declare, is my friend Mrs. Snail,
    As busy as ever, I see!"

"Come in, Mrs. Snail," said the little Black Ant,
    "Come join our small party to-night!
Here's the Beetle and Cricket all quite snug and dry,
    And the Glow-worm to give us some light!"

So the Snail came and joined them, still knitting away,
    And the Cricket her fiddle got out;
And then—well, you just should have seen how they danced,
    How they jumped and all capered about!

The Little Black Ant did a skirt-dance quite well;
   The Beetle a gay Highland fling;
And as for the Glow-worm, he just jigged about,
   And *danced* really nothing at all.

But all of a sudden a croaking was heard,
   And who should appear but a Toad,
Who hoarsely demanded their business, and why
   They were all gathered in her abode?

Then what a commotion! The little Black Ant
   Went from one fainting fit to another;
The Snail simply shut herself up in her house,
   And thought she'd escape all the bother!

The Beetle and Glow-worm soon took themselves off,
   And the Cricket and Ant with them too,
And once more these poor creatures were out in the rain,
   And didn't know what they should do.

But they presently came to the trunk of a tree,
   And there they all stayed for the night;
But they never forgot that old, cross Mrs. Toad,
   Who gave them so dreadful a fright!"

"Mrs. Toad certainly succeeded in raising quite a disturbance," your Aunt Amy said, feeling it necessary to make some comment, and Mrs. Mouser replied thoughtfully:

Mr. Thomas Cat's Narrow Escape

"Yes, almost as much as Mr. Man did when he tried to drown Mr. Thomas Cat the other day. It seems that Mr. Thomas had been out in the stable stealing the food which was left for Mr. Towser, and one of the maids, seeing it, told Mr. Man, so then and there it was decided that Mr. Thomas must be drowned. Mr. Man called him up, as if he was the best friend he ever had, and when Mr. Thomas got near enough, he caught him by the tail, starting off at once for the stream.

"'What are you going to do with me?' Mr. Thomas cried, and Mr. Man said:

"'You wait and see. I'll teach you to steal Mr. Towser's food! You are no good, that's what's the trouble with you—you are no good!'

"So he took a rope out of his pocket and tied it around Mr. Thomas' neck, after they got near the water. Then bent down over the bank to get a big rock, when his foot slipped, and in he went splashing and howling until you might have heard him on the next farm, for he couldn't swim a stroke, and the water was deep where he went in.

"Of course Mr. Thomas wasn't able to do anything to help him, so off he started for the house the best he knew how, with the rope dragging on behind, and when he got there, Mrs. Man couldn't help seeing him. Knowing what her husband had counted on doing she mistrusted that something was wrong, so down she ran to the stream, getting there just in time to pull Mr. Man out of the water before he drew his last breath.

"'How did you know where I was?' Mr. Man asked after the water had run out of his mouth.

"'Why the cat just the same as told me, when he came back with a rope around his neck.'

"'Well, he was some good after all,' Mr. Man said.' I had begun to think all cats were useless, but it seems Mr. Crow was right in that poetry of his, after all.'

"Then Mr. Man went up to the house, and since then Mr. Thomas has been allowed to stay round the farm, just as he pleases."

Mr. Crow's Fancy

"What did he mean by saying Mr. Crow was right?"

"Oh, that was on account of a piece of poetry he wrote about me. There isn't much of it, and perhaps you had just as soon I would repeat it."

Then, without waiting for permission, Mrs. Mouser recited the following:

Some people love the gay giraffe
Because his antics make them laugh
    (I've never found him witty),
Others prefer the cockatoo—
He does things I should hate to do;
    He's vulgar—more's the pity!

An ostrich draws admiring throngs
Whenever he sings his comic songs,
    And, really, it's no wonder!
The dormouse has been highly rated
(and justly) for his celebrated
    Mimicking of thunder.

I know some friends who'd journey miles
To see a bat's face wreathed in smiles,
    They say it's grandly funny!

To see a buzzard drink port wine
Another eager friend of mine
    Would pay no end of money.

But that which most appeals to me—
I know my taste may curious be—
    Is—not a mouse in mittens.
It is to see a homely cat,
Dressed up in an old battered hat,
    A-walking with her kittens!

"One would think from the verses, that you and Mr. Crow were very good friends," your Aunt Amy suggested, and Mrs. Mouser said with a purr of content:

"We have always got along very well together, and I hope we always shall, for really, say what you please about that old bird, it wouldn't be pleasant to have him making sport of you in his verses. We are neither of us as much in love with ourselves as were the peacock and the crane, therefore I don't fancy we shall ever have any very serious trouble."

A Question of Beauty

"What about the peacock and the crane?" your Aunt Amy asked, not disposed to let slip any opportunity of hearing a story.

"Oh, that's something very, very old—why, my grandmother used to tell about it. You know the crane thinks he has got a pretty tail, and I'm not saying anything against it, for it is handsome; but this crane my grandmother used to tell about, had the idea that he was the finest looking bird who ever came out of an egg. He went around making a good deal of such talk as that, and one day he met with a peacock for the first time. Strangely enough, he had never heard about such a bird, so he strutted back and forth as usual, and after they had talked a while of the weather, and all that sort of thing, Mr. Crane said:

"'People tell me I am one of the handsomest birds that ever lived. There's nothing in this world that quite comes up to my tail feathers, and that much I can say without risk of being thought vain.'

"'You have some very pretty feathers,' Mr. Peacock said, keeping his own tail folded up so it couldn't be seen very well. 'But do you really think they are more beautiful than can be found on any other bird?'

"'I don't *think* so, I know it,' Mr. Crane said, spreading the long plumes of his tail out so they would show to the best advantage, and just then Mr. Peacock unfolded his tail to its full size.

"If you ever saw an astonished bird, it was Mr. Crane. He looked at the beautiful feathers spread out like a great, big fan, and then started to fly away.

"'Where are you going?' Mr. Peacock asked.

"And Mr. Crane answered, while he was in the air:

"'Off somewhere to hide until I have got sense enough to hold my tongue when I don't know what I'm talking about.'

"Since that time I have never heard any of the cranes doing very much bragging, and it is a pity that there are yet others around this place who ought to get just such a lesson, for many of the animals here need it sadly."

"You among the rest?" your Aunt Amy asked laughingly, and Mrs. Mouser Cat replied:

"Thank goodness, I am not proud, and perhaps it is because I haven't very much to take pride in. But I have lived long enough in this world to know that one of us is of just about as much importance as another, and the animal or the bird who thinks this world couldn't move very well without him, is making a big mistake. There is nobody whose place cannot be filled when it becomes necessary; there would even be somebody to run this farm as well as Mr. Man does, if he should die to-morrow."

Menagerie Poetry

"What I have in mind is told, in a foolish kind of a way, I suppose, by Mr. Crow, who wrote the verses when Mr. Man's little girl Dolly wanted a pet, and no matter how much she thought of one, if it died, or got lost, the next that came along suited her almost as well.

"Of course I don't want you to suppose I think this is anything but nonsense; but at the same time it carries out the idea of what I have been trying to say," and then Mrs. Mouser repeated the following:

I once possessed an Elephant
    Who fed on potted grouse;
One day I lost him, but I think
    He's somewhere in the house.

I had a Hippopotamus
    Who really was quite slim;
He caught a chill, and so I thought
    I'd best get rid of him.

I also had a gay Giraffe,
    Whose antics made me wince;
He went a walk to Brooklyn town,
    I've never seen him since.

The Puffing Fish that I possessed
    Would fill my heart with pride;
But ah! one day I made a joke—
    He laughed so that he died.

You should have seen my Polar Bear,
    He was a lively beast;
But what became of him at last
    I've no idea, the least.

My Grizzly Bear was certainly
    By all my friends admired.
He tried to climb the Monument,
    And when he failed, expired.

Perhaps the dearest of them all
    Was James, my Cockatoo—
He took to stopping out at nights;
    I gave him to the Zoo

So now I haven't anything;
    It's lonely, I must own.
I'll get a little calf, I think—
    I cannot live alone!

"I don't wonder you call that 'Menagerie Poetry,'" your Aunt Amy said when Mrs. Mouser ceased speaking; "but I think I understood, even without the aid of the verses, the moral you intended to draw."

"I should hope you did; but I remembered those lines, and it seemed to me they came in just right. There is a story he tells about the Elephant and the Bee, which teaches the same kind of a lesson."

When Mr. Elephant and Mr. Bee Had a Quarrel

"I certainly would like to hear it," your Aunt Amy said when Mrs. Mouser Cat ceased speaking, as if waiting for some such permission.

"Well, in the first place you must understand that there was once an Elephant and a Bee that were the very best of friends," Mrs. Mouser Cat said as she curled her tail around her fore paws to prevent them from being chilled by the draft. "One day the Elephant had walked a long distance, and thought he would sit down to rest for a little while. Now it seems the Bee had been flying around there, and he had got tired too, so he laid down on the grass and went to sleep.

"Now what do you think? When Mr. Elephant sat down he happened to hit Mr. Bee's hind foot, and then there was a time! Mr. Bee talked disgracefully, so it is said, to Mr. Elephant, and you would have thought they never had been friends; but Mr. Elephant didn't answer him back, because he was a peaceable kind of an animal, and knew that the least said is the soonest mended.

"When Mr. Bee got through scolding, they went on their journey again. I don't know where they were traveling, but that doesn't make any difference in the story. Off they started, and after a while it seemed as if Mr. Bee got to feeling better, and Mr. Elephant said:

"'I'm glad to see that you've got over being cross, for it was all an accident, my hitting your foot.'

"'Oh yes,' Mr. Bee answered, as if he intended to be friendly again. 'We'll try to forget all about it. Have you seen anything of my collars and cuffs since we started?'

"'Why, no,' replied Mr. Elephant. 'Have you lost them?'

"'I haven't seen them since we left home, and I believe they must be in your trunk.'

"'I think not,' Mr. Elephant said; 'but you can go in and look for them, if you choose.'

"Now Mr. Bee hadn't got over his cross fit a little bit, and he was only waiting for a chance to pay Mr. Elephant back. Well, he crawled into the trunk just as far as he could get, and then he gave poor Mr. Elephant the very hardest sting you ever dreamed about.

"'Oh me, oh my!' Mr. Elephant howled. 'What a wicked little thing you are! I'll fix you for that!' and then he hunched himself together, and gave the biggest kind of a big sneeze. Now if you never saw anything of the kind, you can't have an idea what a commotion it made when Mr. Elephant did that, and, bless your heart, that was the last of Mr. Bee. I don't know what became of him, and neither does anybody else. He must have been dashed to pieces in the terrible wind that was raised, and it served him good and right, too, for he deserved it just as much as ever Mr. Bear did when he got so worn out by Mr. Man's boy Tommy."

When Tommy Got the Best of Mr. Bear

"Is that another story?" your Aunt Amy asked, and Mrs. Mouser replied with a laugh:

"Yes, and it is a good one, too. Last year there was an old Mr. Bear living near this farm, who was the most quarrelsome animal you ever saw, and besides that, he was wicked. Do you know, he made up his mind that he would bite a big piece out of Mr. Man's boy's leg, just because Tommy drove him away when he was stealing honey. So one night he crept up to the well, and got into the bucket, letting himself way down to the bottom where he could float around until Tommy came out to get a pail of water.

"'I'll have him sure,' Mr. Bear said to himself, 'for when he pulls up the bucket in the morning, I'll jump out and grab him, so he can't get away.'

"Well, Tommy went to the well at just about the same time as usual, and when he started to raise the bucket with the windlass, he found it was terribly heavy. He thought some one must have been putting rocks in it to play a joke on him, so he kept on turning the crank around until the bucket was nearly to the top, and then he saw what was the matter:

"'My goodness!' he cried. 'There's Mr. Bear, and it's water I'm after, not bear!'

"Then Tommy Man let go of the windlass, and of course down went Mr. Bear to the bottom of the well with a bump that nearly shook him to pieces.

"Now almost anybody might have thought that Tommy would run away after that; but no, he made up his mind to serve Mr. Bear out good and hard, so he went to work winding up the windlass again. Then, when he had hauled Mr. Bear nearly to the top, he let him go back with a worse bump than before, and so he kept on doing this same thing thirteen or fifteen times, until Mr. Bear was so sore and bruised that he couldn't do much of anything more than hold himself on to the edge of the bucket.

"By that time Tommy had got all the sport he wanted, and he let Mr. Bear crawl out of the bucket. I have heard it said that it was more than two weeks before the old fellow could get out of bed, and the lesson did him as much good as the one Mr. Donkey gave the Wild Hog, for he wasn't quarrelsome again, and behaved himself decently well forever after."

Mr. Donkey's Lesson in Good Manners

"I think the story about the donkey must be one which I have never heard," your Aunt Amy said. "Although the animals on the farm have told me quite a lot about Mr. Donkey, I have never thought of him as a teacher.

"It isn't what you might rightly call a story; but only something that happened when Mr. Donkey showed his good sense. Now I don't understand why Mr. Man tells about any one being as stupid as a donkey. Why, our Neddy is as wise as anybody on this farm, and you will think so when I have told this story about him.

"It was one night after supper, and he thought he would take a stroll up the road, because he hadn't been working very hard that day, and the exercise might do him good. He was going along, minding his own business, when Mr. Wild Hog came out from the bushes, and into the road.

"Mr. Donkey stepped over one side so as to give him plenty of room, saying 'good evening' politely, and was walking on when Mr. Wild Hog bristled up to him, showing both his big tusks, and said:

"'Why don't you turn out when you meet anybody of consequence?'

"'Perhaps I do when I meet them,' Mr. Donkey replied, and that made Mr. Hog terribly angry. "'Do you know I have a mind to give you a lesson in good manners?' growled Mr. Hog, and Mr. Donkey said with a grin:

"'Why not go off somewhere alone, and give yourself a lesson or two?'

"Of course that made Mr. Hog more angry than ever, and he said:

"'Do you know what I do when stupid animals like you try to be too smart?'

156

"'No; I don't care either,' Mr. Donkey replied; 'but I will show you what I do when animals make bigger hogs of themselves than is natural.'

"Just as he said this he turned around, swung up both heels, struck Mr. Hog under the chin, and knocked him over and over as many as six times. Then Mr. Donkey trotted off slowly, with a smile on his face that was for all the world like Mr. Crocodile's after he had been to the dentist's."

When Mr. Crocodile Had His Teeth Extracted

"Why did he go to the dentist?" your Aunt Amy asked, thinking to hear another story.

"I had better repeat the poetry Mr. Crow wrote about it, for that tells the whole story, and without further delay Mrs. Mouser Cat recited the following:

Come, listen, and I'll sing awhile
    About a winsome crocodile,
Who had a most engaging smile
    Whene'er he smole.
His basket with fresh fish to fill
    Each day he'd tramp o'er vale and hill,
For he possessed quite wondrous skill
    With rod and pole.

But as he fished, one summer's day,
    A toothache chased his smiles away;
No longer could he fish and play
    His favorite role.

He stamped and growled, the pain was vile,
    No more he grinned, Sir Crocodile,
(And he'd a most engaging smile
    Whene'er he smole.)

So straight he to the dentist went,
    On stopping or extraction bent,
His soul was with such anguish rent;
    He reached his goal.

"Come sit down in the chair awhile;
    Open your mouth, Sir Crocodile!"
(He had a most engaging smile
    Whene'er he smole.)

"Which is the tooth?" the dentist said;
    "Dear, dear! You must have suffered—
You've not a sound tooth in your head,
    Not one that's whole!"

He pulled them out; it took some while,
    And then that toothsome crocodile
Had not quite such a pleasing smile
    Whene'er he smole.

"How do you suppose Mr. Crocodile felt when he was hungry, and wanted to eat something?" your Aunt Amy asked.

The Dissatisfied Cat

"Most likely much the same as did old Mrs. Pussy Cat up on the next farm."

"How was that?" your Aunt Amy asked.

"Well, you see, she was partly black and partly white, and not being a very neat cat, the white hair got dirty so often that she believed it would be a great thing if it was all black. So she got the idea into her head that if she should shave off the white hair, it would be the color she wanted when it grew out again.

"Well, now what do you suppose that poor foolish thing did? Why she went to the barber's, and had him shave all the white hair off of her body. She actually frightened the ducks and the geese when she came home, she looked so queer; but you couldn't have made her believe it. She thought she was a perfect beauty, and when she came over to this farm that evening, Mr. Thomas Cat said to her:

"'Why you are a perfect sight, that's what you are, with those tufts of black hair all over you!'

"'That's all the style,' Mrs. Pussy Cat said, and I think she really believed that she was as handsome as any cat you could find.

"Well, things went along all right while the weather was warm, but in the course of ten days we had a heavy frost, and dear me, dear me, how cold it grew all of a sudden! Poor Mrs. Pussy Cat was almost frozen to death the first night of the cold snap, when she tried to stay with the rest of us to a concert, and went home moaning:

"'Oh, give me back my hair! Give me back my hair!'

"Of course that couldn't be done, because she had to wait for it to grow again; but Mrs. Man on the next farm wrapped her up in an old shawl, and she had to stay in a basket until her hair grew, else she'd have frozen to death, for we had a terrible hard winter that season. When the hair did come out it was uneven, of course, and she was the worst looking cat you ever saw.

"Mr. Man was shaving the first morning Mrs. Pussy Cat came out of the basket, and he hadn't seen her since she had been to the barber's.

"She jumped up on a chair by the side of him, thinking he would stroke her fur as he always used to do, when the poor man got one glimpse of her, and it nearly scared him into hysterics. I suppose he thought it was a ghost, or something like that, for she looked bad enough to be almost anything.

"He gave a yell, and jumped in the air. That scared Mrs. Pussy Cat, and she screamed as she leaped out of the chair. Then Mr. Man went after her with that big razor in his hand.

"I don't know how far he chased her; but Mr. Towser said that Mrs. Pussy Cat ran more than five miles before she stopped, and when she sneaked back home that night, I'm thinking she felt a good deal as Mr. Crow did when he tried to make folks believe peacock feathers were growing in his tail."

Mr. Crow's Deceit

"I have heard a great many stories which Mr. Crow has told; but never one about him," your Aunt Amy interrupted. "If he tried to deceive the other birds, I surely would like to know about it."

"Well, he did," Mrs. Mouser Cat said emphatically, sitting bolt upright; "but of course he doesn't like to have the story told, so I had rather you wouldn't let him know I mentioned it.

"I don't know how he happened to get it into his head to do such a thing, for, as a rule, he spends the most of his time over in the big tree telling stories or making poetry; but he grew foolish once, and whenever anybody came where he was, he said he had strange growing feathers, and the doctor believed he was turning into a peacock.

"Of course that made a good deal of excitement around here, among all of us, for it would be a strange thing for a crow to change in that way, and he had twice as many visitors as he ever had before, all wanting to know about the new feathers.

"Well, of course he couldn't keep saying that they were coming, and not show any signs of them, so one day he said he felt terribly sick and guessed he should go into the hospital. Then we didn't see anything of him for most a week, until little Redder Squirrel came around and said Mr. Crow was all right; that he had as many as six peacock feathers growing right out of his tail.

"Well, now, you can believe we were astonished, and more excited over it than we had been since young Mr. Thomas Cat painted the canary yellow. Of course we asked Redder Squirrel where we could see him, and he said Mr. Crow had agreed to come out on the hill, just under the tree, that afternoon.

"If we animals around here were anxious to see him, you can guess that the peacocks were just about wild, and when the time came for Mr. Crow to show himself, all the peacocks for as many as five miles around were gathered under the big tree. Mr. Crow didn't know anything about their coming, until he marched right out in the midst of them.

"Now Mr. Crow is really a wise bird, and how it happened that he was so foolish as to do what he did, beats me. Anybody with half an eye could see that he had simply stuck these feathers in his tail, and was trying to make us believe they had grown there. If he had stayed on the tree where we couldn't get very near him, there might have been some chance of deceiving us; but there he was right down where we could put our paws on him if we wanted to. And the peacocks! Angry? Oh me, oh my, don't say a word!

"One big one reached over with his beak, and pulled a feather from Mr. Crow's tail.

"'The next time you set yourself up for one of us, it would be a good idea to tie the feathers in, else they may drop out, as this one has,' the peacock said, and I expected to see Mr. Crow almost faint away with shame. But bless you, he never thought of doing anything of that kind. He took the feather as bold as a lion, looked at the end of it, and then he said, careless-like:

"'Well, I declare! I guess I must be moulting,' and with that, off he flew. We didn't see him again for as much as two weeks, and then he agreed not to write any poetry about us if we wouldn't tell the story of the feathers; but young Mr. Thomas Cat couldn't hold in, and reported it far and near, till Mr. Crow paid him back in good shape."

When Young Thomas Cat Painted a Canary

"But what about painting a canary?" your Aunt Amy asked. "You spoke of such a thing a moment ago."

"Yes, and it is what I am telling you about. Mr. Crow wrote the poetry which tells the story, and you shall hear it."

Then Mrs. Mouser Cat repeated the following:

For he was such a knowing puss—
  Oh yes, he was!
A really clever, sharp young puss—
  Oh yes, he was!
He wouldn't do as others do,
He said, "I know a thing or two,
  I do!

"To-morrow is the great bird show—
    I think it is;
The far-renowned canary show—
    Of course it is.
Some yellow ochre, so I've heard,
Will wondrously improve a bird,
    I've heard

"I think I'll enter at that show—
    I think I will,
Just make one entry for that show—
    By Jove, I will.
And if my bird don't get the prize,
Why it will be, as I surmise,
    A surprise!"
The show was held—a great success—
    Of course it was!
By all 'twas called a huge success—
    Indeed it was!
The judges were experienced cats;
They wore tail-coats, and large top-hats—
    Such hats!

Young Tom was there—he'd brought his bird—
    Just think! he had!
He'd really dared to bring that bird—
    Oh yes, he had!
He said, "No one will ever know
That my canary's all no go,
    Oh no!"

But one old judge was rather spry—
    Oh yes, he was!
You'd not have thought him half so spry,
    But oh, he was!
He said, "Why really, on my word!
Disqualify that shocking bird!—
    Absurd!"

So Tom's bird was disqualified—
    Of course it was!
Disgracefully disqualified,
    Ah yes, it was!
And Tom, although he thought he knew
A thing or two, found others too
    Who knew.

"Mr. Thomas must have believed that honesty was the best policy, before he got through with the bird show," your Aunt Amy suggested, and Mrs. Mouser Cat laughed as she replied:

"It would have shamed almost any cat; but it didn't seem to make a bit of difference with young Thomas. He was just as pert as ever the next day, and went around telling about the prize he would have taken if the judge hadn't discovered the fraud. It would have served him right if he had been punished as was Mr. Fox."

When Mr. Fox Was Too Cunning

"Is that another story?" your Aunt Amy asked.

"Yes, it is," Mrs. Mouser said reflectively, "and it shows that there are times when even a fox can be too cunning. One day while Mr. Fox, who used to live down in the swamp, was sneaking around behind the barn on this farm, he saw a bag hanging on the limb of a tree just over the water barrel.

"'Now I wonder what that is?' he said to himself, as he stopped and looked first at the bag and then at the barrel. 'It smells good, and I believe there's meat somewhere around here.'

"Then he climbed upon the barrel, and saw that it was half full of water, so he began to wonder what the meaning of it was.

"'It must be a trap Mr. Man has set for me,' he said rubbing his ear as if he thought himself very wise. 'He thinks I'll jump up for the bag, and fall into the water. Now he's got to find a younger fox than I am, if he wants to make that plan work, for I'm going to know what's hanging up there, and I won't take any chances of getting drowned, either, because I'll drink all the water first. Then that will settle it.'

"Well, he began to drink, and drink, and drink, until he swelled up amazingly; but there was plenty of water still left in the barrel. Then he drank some more; ran around a few moments, came back and drank again, until he was all swelled out, and couldn't swallow another drop; but the barrel appeared to be as full as when he commenced.

"By this time it wasn't possible for him to run the least little bit, and he was feeling a good deal as his father did after he had found the crab, when along came Mr. Man, who said:

"'Hello! here's a nice fat fox! I guess I'll take his skin,' and the next day, lo and behold, there was Mr. Fox's hide nailed up on the barn, showing that sometimes it is dangerous to be too cunning."

When Sonny Bunny Rabbit Was Rash

"I never saw an animal who didn't get into trouble when he thought he knew everything," Mrs. Mouser went on thoughtfully, giving no heed to the fact that your Aunt Amy was on the point of interrupting her. "Now there is Sonny Bunny Rabbit, he got it into his head that he was the greatest ever lived; that he could do just as he wanted to around this neighborhood, because he led Mr. Fox into a trap one day.

"Why, that foolish little rabbit used to sit out in the field at night, and tell me, who am old enough to be his grandmother at the very least, that he could do anything he pleased; that there was no animal around here who could get the best of him.

"Well, Sonny Bunny kept that idea in his mind, and one day Mr. Hawk came sailing along just when Sonny Bunny was talking with Redder Squirrel, and Redder he screamed:

"'Run, Sonny Bunny! Run for your life!'

"'You don't catch me running away from any old hawk,' Sonny Bunny said, as bold as a lion. 'I'm going to stay right here, and kick dirt in his face if he comes where I am.'

"'Run, Sonny Bunny, run!' Redder Squirrel cried, and for once he showed more sense than usual.

"But Sonny Bunny was so puffed up with what he thought he could do, that he stood still, and got ready to kick dirt, while old Mr. Hawk came sailing round, and round, and round, making ready to light on him. If you'll believe it, that foolish rabbit stayed right there until down came Mr. Hawk, and then, oh me, oh my, how Sonny did kick dirt!

"I'm willing to admit that part of his plan was all right. He blinded Mr. Hawk, but at the same time didn't save all of his own skin, for the old fellow's claws went into Sonny Bunny's back so far, as his mother told me, that you could almost see the bones, and the foolish rabbit laid in bed three or four weeks before he was fit to go out of doors again."

"It seems to me as if I had heard something like that before," your Aunt Amy said, and Mrs. Mouser replied:

"Very likely you've heard the same story, for all the animals around here know about it."

"But what was it you said about Mr. Fox's father meeting a crab?" your Aunt Amy asked.

Mr. Fox and Miss Crab

"Well, that isn't what you might really call a story; it's only something which happened to old Mr. Fox when he went down to the seashore for his health, and met young Miss Crab. He had never seen anybody of the kind, and didn't know whether she was an animal, or a fish, or a bird.

"'Good morning,' he said very politely, and Miss Crab answered him back as nice as you please.

"'Are you out for a walk?' he asked.

"'Oh no, indeed,' she said. 'I am here taking the sea air for my health. The doctor recommends it, but I am not allowed to move around very much because I'm so feeble.'

"Now old Mr. Fox was puzzled. He put his paw on her shell, and it was hard; but whether it was the house she lived in, or a part of herself, he couldn't for the life of him tell.

"Well, after a time he made up his mind that the shell must be her house, so he said:

"'Why don't you come outside where you can get purer air than you do in there?' and she replied, just as a gull went sailing by:

"'I don't dare to for fear some of those rude birds will eat me.'

"That settled old Mr. Fox. He thought if the birds liked Miss Crab well enough to eat her, she would make a good supper for him. So he began to coax and coax her to come out, and after a long time, finding that she would not do as he wanted, he began trying to bite the shell into pieces. Then she caught hold of his tongue with one of her big claws, and bit as much as an inch and a half right straight off the end of it.

"Oh me, oh my, how old Mr. Fox did howl! I'm told that he went home in a most dreadful rage, with the blood streaming out of his mouth, and when his wife asked him what the matter was, he couldn't say a word, of course not, because his tongue was gone. I don't know how long it was before he got well; but they do say he was the most shamefaced looking animal that was ever seen, whenever any one spoke to him about crabs, or the seashore."

The Baby Elephant

"Speaking of the seashore reminds me of another piece of Mr. Crow's poetry, and if you can stand any more, I wish you would, because I think this is really good."

As a matter of course your Aunt Amy could do no less than say she would be pleased to hear it, and Mrs. Mouser recited that which is set down here:

To little John Adolphus Chubb
    Your kind attention I invite;
Oh, how he loves to bathe and scrub,
    Each day at noon and eke at night.

Now John Adolphus William Chubb
    A fine young elephant is he;
And when he's in his little tub,
    Oh, 'tis a pleasant sight to see!

His nurse,—a motherly old thing—
    No need to coax the rogue has she;
Adolphus, when he sees her bring
    The water, trumpets in his glee.

Oh, how he loves the cold, cold stream
    Descending on him in the tub!
He feels as if he'd like to scream—
    He loves it so—does William Chubb.

And then, the evening's washing o'er
    (Though he could wish it lasted still),
His nurse will gay, "Come, come, no more;
    You've had enough now, Master Will!"

So swift he's dried, his night-gown on,
    A night-cap tied upon his head,
And to the rattle's music,
    John Adolphus William goes to bed.

"I don't think that is very nice poetry," your Aunt Amy said when Mrs. Mouser had come to the end of the verses. "It is too ridiculous."

"That may be; but I have heard some of your friends, like Mr. Turtle, for example, tell you even worse than that," and Mrs. Mouser spoke quite sharply. "Now if you want a really pretty little story, that hasn't got much fun in it, I can tell you one about two mice, and it must be true, because I had it from a cat friend of mine who was on the spot."

The Story of Squeaky Mouse

Your Aunt Amy said to Mrs. Mouser that she would be very much pleased to hear it, and, telling the story as if she did not entirely approve of it herself, Mrs. Mouser began:

"Mother Mouse had two little daughters, Meeky and Squeaky. Meeky was a good little mouse, and did everything her mother told her. Squeaky was very brave and daring, but she was the torment of everybody's life.

"One day Mother Mouse was too ill to go out and do her own marketing.

"'I wish you children would go and get me a little lump of cheese,' she moaned.

"Away scampered the two little mice to a high shelf they knew of; their mother had warned them against traps and cats, so they were careful not to linger on the pantry floor. When they found the cheese, Meeky began at once rolling up a little lump to take home to her mother, but Squeaky filled her mouth as full as it would hold, and ran up and down the shelf, making a great clatter.

"'Be careful,' said her sister. 'The cat will hear you.'

"Squeaky looked down and saw the cat on the pantry shelf; she knew it couldn't get up to her, and she could not resist calling:

"'Peekaboo!'

"Dear me, how Mrs. Cat glared!

"'Oh,' said Meeky, 'how are we to get down with mother's cheese now?'

"Squeaky said they would wait till the cat went to sleep, and pretty soon this seemed to be the case. But Mrs. Cat was only shamming, for the minute Squeaky reached the floor she pounced upon her, and while the mouse was carried shrieking away, Meeky made her escape.

"Of course, Mother Mouse and Meeky felt badly for a while, but the other mice said it was just what might have been expected, and just what happened to young mice who would not mind what their elders told them."

"Don't you ever feel badly, Mrs. Mouser, when you have caught a mouse, to think that it had a mother, and brothers and sisters, in its hole, waiting for it to come back?" your Aunt Amy asked.

"Why should I?" and Mrs. Cat spoke sharply. "Mice were made for cats to eat, and even if they were not, unless I killed all I could, Mr. Man's house would be over-run with them."

A Saucy Mouse

"Of course I can't do very much in the daytime, because they don't come out of their holes; but I work all night, and it would surprise you to know how many there are in the house, I don't kill off a tenth part of them, and they seem to think they have more rights here than I have.

"Why, it is only last week that I happened to look up on the broad shelf in the dining-room closet, and there were six mice, sitting around as bold as you please. Five ran for their lives the minute they saw me; but what do you think the other one did? Why, he sat on his tail with his paws behind him, and actually scolded because I had come around there.

"I really believe the foolish creature thought he could frighten me, for he kept right on scolding and sputtering until I got my paw on his neck, and of course that settled him. I left him a good deal worse off than Mrs. Lioness did Mr. Rat, when she wanted to play with him."

Fatal Sport

"That must be a new story," your Aunt Amy said, and Mrs. Mouser looked surprised as she replied:

"Well, well, I don't understand what all the animals around here have talked about! This is the third or fourth very old story that you haven't heard, and when I came in here to visit this afternoon, I had an idea that everything I might offer to tell, you had heard from some of the others."

"Suppose you tell me what Mrs. Lioness did to Mr. Rat?" your Aunt Amy suggested, and Mrs. Mouser began:

"Once upon a time—you can see from the beginning how old this story is—Mr. Rat ate his way into the place where they keep animals to show them off—a Zoological Garden, I believe Mr. Man calls it. Well, after Mr. Rat got in he found a Mrs. Lion who was all alone, and feeling as though she really needed company. She was just as kind to Mr. Rat as she could be, and asked him why he didn't make his home there with her.

"'I would like to,' Mr. Rat said, 'for you seem to be a very nice kind of a Mrs. Lion; but when Mr. Man, who owns this place, comes along, he will kill me if he can.'

"'I would like to see Mr. Man try to hurt any one who was visiting me!' Mrs. Lion said sharply, as she held up her paw. 'Do you see that? I could kill Mr. Man with it in a minute if I struck him.'

"As she spoke she laid her paw on Mr. Rat in play, just to show him what she could do, and the 'play' was so rough that the breath of life was squeezed out of Mr. Rat in a jiffy.

"Now you might have supposed that Mrs. Lion would feel badly because she had killed Mr. Rat without meaning to; but instead of that she said, looking at his body:

"'What a poor kind of a creature he must be, when he allows himself to be killed with what was no more than a love pat!'

"And a little mouse, who was sitting in a hole in the wall, having seen all that happened, squeaked with a nervous snicker:

"'A lion's sport is altogether too strenuous for such as us, and if Mr. Rat had been wise, he would have kept well outside the cage, fearing your play even more than your anger,' said Mrs. Lion.

"'It seems to me he was a wise little mouse,' your Aunt Amy said, and Mrs. Mouser replied with a sneer:

"He was a good deal like many others I know of, exceeding wise after they have seen the result of another's folly. But it seems to me that we are talking altogether too much about mice."

A Cat's Dream

"I have been wanting to repeat to you what I call some very nice poetry, which Mr. Crow made about a dream of mine. It is really the best thing he ever wrote, and although I the same as promised not to ask you to listen to anything more of his, I am very anxious for you to hear it."

"Don't think that I object so severely to what Mr. Crow writes," your Aunt Amy replied. "I have heard a number of things he wrote which I thought were very good indeed."

Then Mrs. Mouser Cat repeated the following:

Kitty cat, kitty cat, asleep on the rug,
With velvet paws beneath your head nice and snug,
What are you dreaming of? What do you think
When out slips your little tongue so soft and pink?

When you flick your ears, and your whiskers quiver so,
And you give an eager cry like a whisper low;
When your tail pats the rug so intent, and you seem
Just ready for a spring, tell me what do you dream?

"Oh, I have a fairy-land I visit in my sleep,
Where the mice don't expect me and are playing bo-peep;
Down I pounce upon them, they are not so quick as I,
And I smile as I regale myself upon a mouse pie;

"There are pantries where the pans of milk are brimming o'er,
Where I lap the rich cream and spill no drop upon the floor;
Loveliest custards, daintiest bits of fragrant cheese;
And I help myself without a word as often as I please.
"Then I walk along the fences and I grandly wave my tail;
My whiskers are so fierce all the other cats turn pale;
When Pug and Towser eye me, suspiciously, I know,
I give a spring upon them and off in fright they go.

"And in my pretty fairy-land no cruel boys appear;
Only black eats and white cats, and purrs and mews to hear.
And these are what my visions are, oh little mistress sweet;
Sure any cat would need to smile asleep here at your feet."

"Now I really think that is good, Mrs. Mouser," and your
Aunt Amy spoke no more than the truth. "I don't seriously object
to Mr. Crow's nonsense verses; but at the same time I never really
enjoy them."

Blood Relations

"Of course there's a difference in tastes," Mrs. Mouser said thoughtfully. "Some of the things which Bunny Rabbit thinks are good, I don't like at all, and perhaps he objects to what I believe is very fine. Now here is a story Mr. Crow has got about Mr. Man's boy Tommy. Mamma Speckle thinks there was nothing like it ever told. He says that Tommy Man, one night after he had been tucked up in his crib, was awakened by a strange, humming, buzzing sound close to his head, and when he got out the sand that the 'sand-man' had put in his eyes, he stared about him. There on the bottom of the bed was a fearful hobgoblin, so Tommy Man thought, with big round eyes, awfully long legs and wings, and a beak that looked like a trooper's sword.

"'Are you one of those angels that my mamma said took care of little boys at night?' asked Tommy Man, trembling.' 'Cause if you are I guess I can get along by myself all right; you needn't stay.'

"But the mosquito made a jab with his bill at the bed-clothes over Tommy's chin, and said, loudly:

"'Cousin-n-n-n-n, Cousin-n-n-n.'

"'Oh, you're a cousin, are you? I wonder which one?'

"'Z-z-i-m m-m,' answered the mosquito, buzzing about Tommy Man's head.

"'Zim? Oh, I guess you must be that soldier cousin of mother's by the looks of the sword you carry; his name was Jim.'

"'Cousin-n-n-n-n!' buzzed the mosquito sharply. 'Don't you know your own relations?'

"'You my relation?' Tommy asked in amazement. 'How do you make that out?'

"'Oh, easy. Relations are those who have the same blood in them, ain't they?'

"'Yes,' assented Tommy.

"'Well, you and I have the same blood. You had it, and now I've got it. I just tapped you, you know.'

"Tommy didn't know anything of the kind, and he was terribly frightened, so he just covered up his head, and trembled until Mr. Mosquito flew away."

"Those are what I call nonsense stories," your Aunt Amy said when Mrs. Mouser ceased speaking, and she replied quite sharply:

"Of course they are, and that is about all the animals on this farm know."

"I am certain you make a mistake, Mrs. Mouser Cat, for you have told me several this afternoon which teach a good lesson," your Aunt Amy said, and for a moment it seemed very much as if Mrs. Mouser was angry, but her face brightened an instant later, as she cried:

"I've got the very story for you, although it's about a mouse, and I don't really believe in talking of them so much, for it makes it appear as if they were of great importance, when all they are fit for is to furnish food for us cats.

"Once upon a time there was a miller who lived in his mill, and on a certain morning, when he was opening the sacks of grain, out hopped a little mouse.

"'Oh, wife, wife!' he cried as if he had seen some horrible animal. 'Bring me the butcher knife so that I can kill this mouse!'

"But the little mouse put her paws together and begged for her life. She promised to keep the mill free from mice if the miller would spare her life. Well, after a good deal of talk the miller agreed that she should be allowed to live in the mill, and for a whole month she kept her word so well that not even a mouse's tail was seen anywhere around the place. Then, one morning the miller heard a faint squeaking, and he cried out angrily:

"'What's this, Mrs. Mouse? You have forgotten your promise, and let in some of your friends.'

"No,' answered the little mouse, 'I have kept my promise. Those are my three babies, who were born last night,' and she led the way proudly to her nest, where the three squirming little mouse babies lay.

"'So this is the way you keep your word, is it?' the miller cried angrily. 'You promised to drive all other mice away from this mill, and here are three who have come to get their living from me!'

"Then he picked up the babies and threw them into the river. Oh, but the little mouse was angry! Yet she was only a mouse, and he was a man, so she said nothing; but after that, whenever she got a chance, she gnawed and gnawed and gnawed at the outer post of the mill, sometimes working the whole night long.

"Then came a big storm, and the river rose very high; the posts which were half gnawed through, broke, and the mill fell over into the river.

"'Save me! Save me!' shouted the miller as the swiftly-running current carried him down the stream.

"'I am sending you to find my lost babies,' squeaked the little mouse as she ran to and fro on the bank.

"There's a good lesson in that story, if you know how to find it," Mrs. Mouser said as she curled herself into a little ball near the fireplace, much as though she had come to an end of her story-telling; but just at that moment a mouse showed his nose in one corner of the room.

In an instant Mrs. Mouser Cat was on her feet looking as if she had never thought of such a thing as taking a nap, and in a very few seconds she had the mouse in her claws.

"I guess this breaks up my visit," she said, going toward the door. "I must give the kittens a chance to learn how a mouse should be caught, and it isn't likely I'll have time to come back here this afternoon."

Then Mrs. Mouser Cat disappeared through the half-opened door, and your Aunt Amy was left alone, wondering which, of all the animals on the farm, would be the next to provide her with an afternoon's entertainment.

Whittington and His Cat
Joseph Jacobs

In the reign of the famous King Edward III there was a little boy called Dick Whittington, whose father and mother died when he was very young. As poor Dick was not old enough to work, he was very badly off; he got but little for his dinner, and sometimes nothing at all for his breakfast; for the people who lived in the village were very poor indeed, and could not spare him much more than the parings of potatoes, and now and then a hard crust of bread.

Now Dick had heard a great many very strange things about the great city called London; for the country people at that time thought that folks in London were all fine gentlemen and ladies; and that there was singing and music there all day long; and that the streets were all paved with gold.

One day a large wagon and eight horses, all with bells at their heads, drove through the village while Dick was standing by the sign-post. He thought that this wagon must be going to the fine town of London; so he took courage, and asked the wagoner to let him walk with him by the side of the wagon. As soon as the wagoner heard that poor Dick had no father or mother, and saw by his ragged clothes that he could not be worse off than he was, he told him he might go if he would, so off they set together.

So Dick got safe to London, and was in such a hurry to see the fine streets paved all over with gold, that he did not even stay to thank the kind wagoner; but ran off as fast as his legs would carry him, through many of the streets, thinking every moment to come to those that were paved with gold; for Dick had seen a guinea three times in his own little village, and remembered what a deal of money it brought in change; so he thought he had nothing to do but to take up some little bits of the pavement, and should then have as much money as he could wish for.

Poor Dick ran till he was tired, and had quite forgot his friend the wagoner; but at last, finding it grow dark, and that every way he turned he saw nothing but dirt instead of gold, he, sat down in a dark corner and cried himself to sleep.

Little Dick was all night in the streets; and next morning, being very hungry, he got up and walked about, and asked everybody he met to give him a halfpenny to keep him from starving; but nobody stayed to answer him, and only two or three gave him a halfpenny; so that the poor boy was soon quite weak and faint for the want of victuals.

In this distress he asked charity of several people, and one of them said crossly: "Go to work, for an idle rogue." "That I will," says Dick, "I will to go work for you, if you will let me." But the man only cursed at him and went on.

At last a good-natured looking gentleman saw how hungry he looked. "Why don't you go to work my lad?" said he to Dick. "That I would, but I do not know how to get any," answered Dick. "If you are willing, come along with me," said the gentleman, and took him to a hay-field, where Dick worked briskly, and lived merrily till the hay was made.

After this he found himself as badly off as before; and being almost starved again, he laid himself down at the door of Mr.

Fitzwarren, a rich merchant. Here he was soon seen by the cook-maid, who was an ill-tempered creature, and happened just then to be very busy dressing dinner for her master and mistress; so she called out to poor Dick: "What business have you there, you lazy rogue? there is nothing else but beggars; if you do not take yourself away, we will see how you will like a sousing of some dish-water; I have some here hot enough to make you jump."

Just at that time Mr. Fitzwarren himself came home to dinner; and when he saw a dirty ragged boy lying at the door, he said to him: "Why do you lie there, my boy? You seem old enough to work; I am afraid you are inclined to be lazy."

"No, indeed, sir," said Dick to him, "that is not the case, for I would work with all my heart, but I do not know anybody, and I believe I am very sick for the want of food."

"Poor fellow, get up; let me see what ails you." Dick now tried to rise, but was obliged to lie down again, being too weak to stand, for he had not eaten any food for three days, and was no longer able to run about and beg a halfpenny of people in the street. So the kind merchant ordered him to be taken into the house, and have a good dinner given him, and be kept to do what work he was able to do for the cook.

Little Dick would have lived very happy in this good family if it had not been for the ill-natured cook. She used to say: "You are under me, so look sharp; clean the spit and the dripping-pan, make the fires, wind up the jack, and do all the scullery work nimbly, or—" and she would shake the ladle at him. Besides, she was so fond of basting, that when she had no meat to baste, she would baste poor Dick's head and shoulders with a broom, or anything else that happened to fall in her way. At last her ill-usage of him was told to Alice, Mr. Fitzwarren's daughter, who told the cook she should be turned away if she did not treat him kinder.

The behaviour of the cook was now a little better; but besides this Dick had another hardship to get over. His bed stood in a garret, where there were so many holes in the floor and the walls that every night he was tormented with rats and mice. A gentleman having given Dick a penny for cleaning his shoes, he thought he would buy a cat with it. The next day he saw a girl with a cat, and asked her, "Will you let me have that cat for a penny?" The girl said: "Yes, that I will, master, though she is an excellent mouser."

Dick hid his cat in the garret, and always took care to carry a part of his dinner to her; and in a short time he had no more trouble with the rats and mice, but slept quite sound every night.

Soon after this, his master had a ship ready to sail; and as it was the custom that all his servants should have some chance for good fortune as well as himself, he called them all into the parlour and asked them what they would send out.

They all had something that they were willing to venture except poor Dick, who had neither money nor goods, and therefore could send nothing. For this reason he did not come into the parlour with the rest; but Miss Alice guessed what was the matter, and ordered him to be called in. She then said: "I will lay down some money for him, from my own purse;" but her father told her: "This will not do, for it must be something of his own."

When poor Dick heard this, he said: "I have nothing but a cat which I bought for a penny some time since of a little girl."

"Fetch your cat then, my lad," said Mr. Fitzwarren, "and let her go."

Dick went upstairs and brought down poor puss, with tears in his eyes, and gave her to the captain; "For," he said, "I shall now be kept awake all night by the rats and mice." All the company laughed at Dick's odd venture; and Miss Alice, who felt pity for him, gave him some money to buy another cat.

This, and many other marks of kindness shown him by Miss Alice, made the ill-tempered cook jealous of poor Dick, and she began to use him more cruelly than ever, and always made game of him for sending his cat to sea.

She asked him: "Do you think your cat will sell for as much money as would buy a stick to beat you?"

At last poor Dick could not bear this usage any longer, and he thought he would run away from his place; so he packed up his few things, and started very early in the morning, on All-hallows Day, the first of November. He walked as far as Holloway; and there sat down on a stone, which to this day is called "Whittington's Stone," and began to think to himself which road he should take.

While he was thinking what he should do, the Bells of Bow Church, which at that time were only six, began to ring, and their sound seemed to say to him:

"Turn again, Whittington, Thrice Lord Mayor of London."

"Lord Mayor of London!" said he to himself. "Why, to be sure, I would put up with almost anything now, to be Lord Mayor of London, and ride in a fine coach, when I grow to be a man! Well, I will go back, and think nothing of the cuffing and scolding of the old cook, if I am to be Lord Mayor of London at last."

Dick went back, and was lucky enough to get into the house, and set about his work, before the old cook came downstairs.

We must now follow Miss Puss to the coast of Africa. The ship with the cat on board, was a long time at sea; and was at last driven by the winds on a part of the coast of Barbary, where the only people were the Moors, unknown to the English. The people came in great numbers to see the sailors, because they were of different colour to themselves, and treated them civilly; and, when they became better acquainted, were very eager to buy the fine things that the ship was loaded with.

When the captain saw this, he sent patterns of the best things he had to the king of the country; who was so much pleased with them, that he sent for the captain to the palace. Here they were placed, as it is the custom of the country, on rich carpets flowered with gold and silver. The king and queen were seated at the upper end of the room; and a number of dishes were brought in for dinner. They had not sat long, when a vast number of rats and mice rushed in, and devoured all the meat in an instant. The captain wondered at this, and asked if these vermin were not unpleasant.

"Oh yes," said they, "very offensive, and the king would give half his treasure to be freed of them, for they not only destroy his dinner, as you see, but they assault him in his chamber, and even in bed, and so that he is obliged to be watched while he is sleeping, for fear of them."

The captain jumped for joy; he remembered poor Whittington and his cat, and told the king he had a creature on board the ship that would despatch all these vermin immediately. The king jumped so high at the joy which the news gave him, that his turban dropped off his head. "Bring this creature to me," says he; "vermin are dreadful in a court, and if she will perform what you say, I will load your ship with gold and jewels in exchange for her."

The captain, who knew his business, took this opportunity to set forth the merits of Miss Puss. He told his majesty; "It is not very convenient to part with her, as, when she is gone, the rats and mice may destroy the goods in the ship—but to oblige your majesty, I will fetch her."

"Run, run!" said the queen; "I am impatient to see the dear creature."

Away went the captain to the ship, while another dinner was got ready. He put Puss under his arm, and arrived at the place just in time to see the table full of rats. When the cat saw them, she did not wait for bidding, but jumped out of the captain's arms, and in a few minutes laid almost all the rats and mice dead at her feet. The rest of them in their fright scampered away to their holes.

The king was quite charmed to get rid so easily of such plagues, and the queen desired that the creature who had done them so great a kindness might be brought to her, that she might look at her. Upon which the captain called: "Pussy, pussy, pussy!" and she came to him. He then presented her to the queen, who started back, and was afraid to touch a creature who had made such a havoc among the rats and mice. However, when the captain stroked the cat and called: "Pussy, pussy," the queen also touched her and cried: "Putty, putty," for she had not learned English. He then put her down on the queen's lap, where she purred and played with her majesty's hand, and then purred herself to sleep.

The king, having seen the exploits of Mrs. Puss, and being informed that her kittens would stock the whole country, and keep it free from rats, bargained with the captain for the whole ship's cargo, and then gave him ten times as much for the cat as all the rest amounted to.

The captain then took leave of the royal party, and set sail with a fair wind for England, and after a happy voyage arrived safe in London.

One morning, early, Mr. Fitzwarren had just come to his counting-house and seated himself at the desk, to count over the cash, and settle the business for the day, when somebody came tap, tap, at the door. "Who's there?" said Mr. Fitzwarren. "A friend," answered the other; "I come to bring you good news of your ship *Unicorn*." The merchant, bustling up in such a hurry that he forgot his gout, opened the door, and who should he see waiting but the captain and factor, with a cabinet of jewels, and a bill of lading; when he looked at this the merchant lifted up his eyes and thanked Heaven for sending him such a prosperous voyage.

They then told the story of the cat, and showed the rich present that the king and queen had sent for her to poor Dick. As soon as the merchant heard this, he called out to his servants:

"Go send him in, and tell him of his fame;
Pray call him Mr. Whittington by name."

Mr. Fitzwarren now showed himself to be a good man; for when some of his servants said so great a treasure was too much for him, he answered: "God forbid I should deprive him of the value of a single penny, it is his own, and he shall have it to a farthing." He then sent for Dick, who at that time was scouring pots for the cook, and was quite dirty. He would have excused himself from coming into the counting-house, saying, "The room is swept, and my shoes are dirty and full of hob-nails." But the merchant ordered him to come in.

Mr. Fitzwarren ordered a chair to be set for him, and so he began to think they were making game of him, at the same time said to them: "Do not play tricks with a poor simple boy, but let me go down again, if you please, to my work."

"Indeed, Mr. Whittington," said the merchant, "we are all quite in earnest with you, and I most heartily rejoice in the news that these gentlemen have brought you; for the captain has sold your cat to the King of Barbary, and brought you in return for her more riches than I possess in the whole world; and I wish you may long enjoy them!"

Mr. Fitzwarren then told the men to open the great treasure they had brought with them; and said: "Mr. Whittington has nothing to do but to put it in some place of safety."

Poor Dick hardly knew how to behave himself for joy. He begged his master to take what part of it he pleased, since he owed it all to his kindness. "No, no," answered Mr. Fitzwarren, "this is all your own; and I have no doubt but you will use it well."

Dick next asked his mistress, and then Miss Alice, to accept a part of his good fortune; but they would not, and at the same time told him they felt great joy at his good success. But this poor fellow was too kind-hearted to keep it all to himself; so he made a present to the captain, the mate, and the rest of Mr. Fitzwarren's servants; and even to the ill-natured old cook.

After this Mr. Fitzwarren advised him to send for a proper tailor and get himself dressed like a gentleman; and told him he was welcome to live in his house till he could provide himself with a better.

When Whittington's face was washed, his hair curled, his hat cocked, and he was dressed in a nice suit of clothes he was as handsome and genteel as any young man who visited at Mr. Fitzwarren's; so that Miss Alice, who had once been so kind to him, and thought of him with pity, now looked upon him as fit to be her sweetheart; and the more so, no doubt, because Whittington was now always thinking what he could do to oblige her, and making her the prettiest presents that could be.

Mr. Fitzwarren soon saw their love for each other, and proposed to join them in marriage; and to this they both readily agreed. A day for the wedding was soon fixed; and they were attended to church by the Lord Mayor, the court of aldermen, the sheriffs, and a great number of the richest merchants in London, whom they afterwards treated with a very rich feast.

History tells us that Mr. Whittington and his lady liven in great splendour, and were very happy. They had several children. He was Sheriff of London, thrice Lord Mayor, and received the honour of knighthood by Henry V.

He entertained this king and his queen at dinner after his conquest of France so grandly, that the king said "Never had prince such a subject;" when Sir Richard heard this, he said: "Never had subject such a prince."

The figure of Sir Richard Whittington with his cat in his arms, carved in stone, was to be seen till the year 1780 over the archway of the old prison of Newgate, which he built for criminals.

The Cat
Andrew Barton "Banjo" Paterson

Most people think that the cat is an unintelligent animal, fond of ease, and caring little for anything but mice and milk. But a cat has really more character than most human beings, and gets a great deal more satisfaction out of life. Of all the animal kingdom, the cat has the most many-sided character.

He—or she—is an athlete, a musician, an acrobat, a Lothario, a grim fighter, a sport of the first water. All day long the cat loafs about the house, takes things easy, sleeps by the fire, and allows himself to be pestered by the attentions of our womenfolk and annoyed by our children. To pass the time away he sometimes watches a mouse-hole for an hour or two—just to keep himself from dying of ennui; and people get the idea that this sort of thing is all that life holds for the cat. But watch him as the shades of evening fall, and you see the cat as he really is.

When the family sits down to tea, the cat usually puts in an appearance to get his share, and purrs noisily, and rubs himself against the legs of the family; and all the time he is thinking of a fight or a love-affair that is coming off that evening. If there is a guest at table the cat is particularly civil to him, because the guest is likely to have the best of what is going. Sometimes, instead of recognizing this civility with something to eat, the guest stoops down and strokes the cat, and says, "Poor pussy! poor pussy!"

The cat soon tires of that; he puts up his claw and quietly but firmly rakes the guest in the leg.

"Ow!" says the guest, "the cat stuck his claws into me!" The delighted family remarks, "Isn't it sweet of him? Isn't he intelligent? He wants you to give him something to eat."

The guest dares not do what he would like to do—kick the cat through the window—so, with tears of rage and pain in his eyes, he affects to be very much amused, and sorts out a bit of fish from his plate and hands it down. The cat gingerly receives it, with a look in his eyes that says: "Another time, my friend, you won't be so dull of comprehension," and purrs maliciously as he retires to a safe distance from the guest's boot before eating it. A cat isn't a fool—not by a long way.

When the family has finished tea, and gathers round the fire to enjoy the hours of indigestion, the cat slouches casually out of the room and disappears. Life, true life, now begins for him.

He saunters down his own backyard, springs to the top of the fence with one easy bound, drops lightly down on the other side, trots across the right-of-way to a vacant allotment, and skips to the roof of an empty shed. As he goes, he throws off the effeminacy of civilisation; his gait becomes lithe and pantherlike; he looks quickly and keenly from side to side, and moves noiselessly, for he has so many enemies—dogs, cabmen with whips, and small boys with stones.

Arrived on the top of the shed, the cat arches his back, rakes his claws once or twice through the soft bark of the old roof, wheels round and stretches himself a few times; just to see that every muscle is in full working order; then, dropping his head nearly to his paws, he sends across a league of backyards his call to his kindred—a call to love, or war, or sport.

The Cat

Before long they come, gliding, graceful shadows, approaching circuitously, and halting occasionally to reconnoitre—tortoiseshell, tabby, and black, all domestic cats, but all transformed for the nonce into their natural state. No longer are they the hypocritical, meek creatures who an hour ago were cadging for fish and milk. They are now ruffling, swaggering blades with a Gascon sense of dignity. Their fights are grim and determined, and a cat will be clawed to ribbons before he will yield.

Even young lady cats have this inestimable superiority over human beings, that they can work off jealousy, hatred, and malice in a sprawling, yelling combat on a flat roof. All cats fight, and all keep themselves more or less in training while they are young. Your cat may be the acknowledged lightweight champion of his district—a Griffo of the feline ring!

Just think how much more he gets out of his life than you do out of yours—what a hurricane of fighting and lovemaking his life is—and blush for yourself. You have had one little love-affair, and never had a good, all-out fight in your life!

And the sport they have, too! As they get older and retire from the ring they go in for sport more systematically; the suburban backyards, that are to us but dullness indescribable, are to them hunting-grounds and trysting-places where they may have more gallant adventure than ever had King Arthur's knights or Robin Hood's merry men.

Grimalkin decides to kill a canary in a neighbouring verandah. Consider the fascination of it—the stealthy reconnaissance from the top of the fence; the care to avoid waking the house-dog, the noiseless approach and the hurried dash, and the fierce clawing at the fluttering bird till its mangled body is dragged through the bars of the cage; the exultant retreat with the spoil; the growling over the feast that follows. Not the least entertaining part of it is the demure satisfaction of arriving home in time for breakfast and hearing the house-mistress say: "Tom must be sick; he seems to have no appetite."

It is always levelled as a reproach against cats that they are more fond of their home than of the people in it. Naturally, the cat doesn't like to leave his country, the land where all his friends are, and where he knows every landmark. Exiled in a strange land, he would have to learn a new geography, to exploit another tribe of dogs, to fight and make love to an entirely new nation of cats. Life isn't long enough for that sort of thing. So, when the family moves, the cat, if allowed, will stay at the old house and attach himself to the new tenants. He will give them the privilege of boarding him while he enjoys life in his own way. He is not going to sacrifice his whole career for the doubtful reward which fidelity to his old master or mistress might bring.